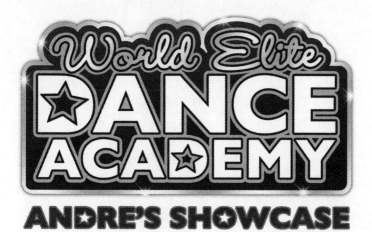

World Elite DANCE ACADEMY

ANDRE'S SHOWCASE

Also available in the WEDA series:

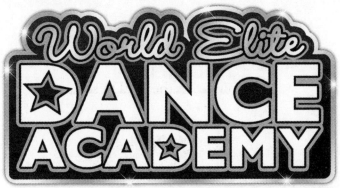

ANDRE'S SHOWCASE

Kimberly Wyatt

EGMONT

EGMONT
We bring stories to life

First published in Great Britain 2017
by Egmont UK Limited
The Yellow Building, 1 Nicholas Road, London W11 4AN

Text copyright © 2017 Beautiful Movements Ltd
Cover illustration copyright © 2017 Beautiful Movements Ltd
Written in collaboration with Siobhan Curham

The moral rights of the author and illustrator have been asserted

ISBN 978 1 4052 8719 7

67253/1

A CIP catalogue record for this title is available
from the British Library

Typeset by Avon DataSet Ltd, Bidford on Avon, Warwickshire
Printed and bound in Great Britain by the CPI Group

MIX
Paper from
responsible sources
FSC® C020471

Dedicated to LaLa Land and the
choreographers that inspired me to believe in me:
Kennis Marquis, Marguerite Derricks, Robin Antin,
Mikey Minden and Brian Friedman.

CHAPTER ONE

Andre stared hard at his phone and began praying to the God of Blogpost Likes (he wasn't exactly sure there *was* a God of Blogpost Likes but he was desperate): *Please, please, please, make more people like my post.*

'Here you go, sweetie – spiralized courgettes, with a tofu Bolognese sauce, topped with grated vegan cheese.'

As Miss Murphy placed Andre's lunch on the table in front of him he glanced up from his phone. 'Thanks, Mum.'

Tofu Bolognese was one of Andre's favourite meals since he'd become vegan but today he couldn't think about the delicious tomato sauce or the way the courgette spaghetti melted in his mouth – nothing could tear his focus from his phone. He looked back at the screen and refreshed the page. His latest post on his fashion blog Spotted still hadn't got any more likes since the initial five. *Why* hadn't it got any more likes? What had he done wrong?

'Is everything OK, my darling?' Miss Murphy sat down at the table opposite him.

'What?' Andre studied the blog post. Maybe he shouldn't have chosen to do a post called 'How to Rock a Pair of Harem Pants'. Maybe it was too niche. Or was it the photos he and Tilly had picked? Maybe they weren't striking enough. He'd read somewhere that fashion blogging was all about the images, that it didn't matter how good the writing was – if the image sucked, no one would bother reading it. 'It's so cray cray!' He sighed.

'Are you all right?' Miss Murphy repeated.

'Yes,' Andre replied, although this was far from true. If his number of likes was dropping then it wouldn't be long before his number of subscribers would too. He was supposed to be *building* a fashion blog, not running it down.

'Well, put the phone away and let's eat,' Miss Murphy said. 'Remember what I said about family time.'

Last week, when Andre had been checking his Instagram likes at the dinner table, his mum had given him a lecture about their Sunday lunches being special. 'It's our only quality time together during the school term,' she'd told him. 'I don't want to be spending it with your phone too.'

Andre knew she had a point. With Miss Murphy's role as Head of Dance and Wellness at the World Elite Dance Academy and Andre being so busy as a student there, plus all his commitments to his street dance crew, Il Bello, and to his fashion blog, they didn't get much time to hang out as mother and son. But what could he do? How else was he going to get the life of his dreams as a super-successful fashion blogger and dancer unless he put the time and work in? As a former world-famous ballerina his mum should have understood this more than anyone. He refreshed the blog page on his phone one more time.

'Andre, we set a strict no-phone rule for this time for the two of us. Get off your phone, honey,' Miss Murphy pleaded.

But Andre could hardly hear his mum he was so far down the wormhole of his online world. 'WHAT, no way!' Andre's heart sank. The number of subscribers to Spotted had gone down by two. *When? How? Why?*

'Andre, put down the phone!' Miss Murphy's softer mum-voice had morphed into her far sterner teacher's voice.

'All right. Geez. No need to yell!' Andre slammed the phone down on the table. This was a disaster. Why had two people unsubscribed? Why, oh why, had he done a post on harem pants?

'Andre!' Miss Murphy stared at him across the table. 'What has gotten into you?'

'Nothing – I . . .' Andre picked up a forkful of courgette spaghetti.

'Are you sure you're OK?' His mum's voice was gentle again, her eyes wide with concern.

'Yeah, I'm fine. Just having a couple of issues with my blog.'

'Hmm.' Miss Murphy frowned. 'Do you really have time to be blogging right now what with all your school work? Maybe you should put the blog on hold for a while.'

Andre looked at her, horrified. Was she crazy? How could she even suggest such a thing? He bet his hero Dr Dre never had to put up with this kind of negative talk when he was his age. 'No! Of course I have time.' He took a deep breath and began speaking slowly and calmly, as though addressing an untrained puppy. 'It's all good, Mum. I just had an issue with my last post, that's all. Let's eat.' He took a mouthful of spaghetti. 'Mmm, this is really good.' The truth was Andre was far too stressed to even notice what he was eating – it was as if dread had destroyed his taste buds – but he couldn't let his mum stop him blogging. That would be the biggest disaster since the death of Tupac.

'Thank you. I have to say I'm really enjoying cooking vegan.' Miss Murphy laughed. 'If your dad could see us now . . .'

Andre stiffened, the way he always did at the mention of his dad. 'What do you mean?'

'Eating vegan food. You know how much he loves a steak.'

'Yeah, the flesh-eating monster. Oh well, I guess it would give him yet another reason to hate on me.'

Miss Murphy's brow furrowed again. 'Your father doesn't hate you.'

'Oh, really?' Andre sighed. He didn't want to have to think about his Neanderthal, steak-loving dad right now – he had way more important things to be worrying about. He wondered if anyone else had unsubscribed from Spotted since he'd last checked, or if he'd got any more likes. His phone buzzed with a notification and he grabbed it.

'Andre. Please.'

He pretended he hadn't heard her. He had received a new email. Someone called @fashattack had commented on the blog post. *Please, please, please let it be something good*, he silently pleaded as he clicked the email open.

I never did get the whole harem pant thing – they make people look like they're wearing giant nappies! Lol ☺

Andre's heart sank. Now people were openly mocking his post. The whole thing was a total disaster. He was in Harem-Pant Hell!

'Andre, for the last time, will you please put down your phone?'

'Sorry, Mum. I thought it might have been an emergency.' He put the phone back on the table.

'A fashion emergency?'

'Yes . . . I mean, no. But you never know, do you, when an emergency might strike. It's always better to be, like, prepared.'

Miss Murphy looked at him like he was the crazy one. And maybe he was – he was certainly starting to feel it.

'Mmm, so delicious,' Andre muttered, shoving half a plateful of spaghetti into his mouth in one go. He needed to get out of his mum's apartment and back to his dorm room where he could figure out how to put things right on Spotted in peace.

Fifteen minutes later, and with painful indigestion from eating so quickly, Andre was back in his room. He opened his laptop and logged on to Spotted. He'd got a handful more likes since he'd last checked but the number was way lower than he normally received. And there was still only one comment – the snarky one about the nappies. Maybe he should delete it. No, if he did that it would be even more embarrassing. It would look like he couldn't take criticism. And he, Andre Murphy, was brave enough to take criticism. He looked at his reflection in the wardrobe mirror and pulled himself upright into what he called his Statue of Liberty pose. He pursed his lips as he gazed admiringly at his fuchsia-pink vest top and ripped skinny jeans and at the way the gold trim on his high-tops perfectly matched the gold flecks in his hoodie. His look was f-e-t-c-h. It always was. He wasn't going to let one snarky comment get to him. He couldn't afford to. There were so many other things he had to think about – like his dance classes at WEDA and what to do with Il Bello next and his academic work and his History homework . . .

Oh shoot! My History homework! He stared at the heap of harem pants on top of his desk. Somewhere buried beneath them was an assignment that had to be done by tomorrow.

Andre made his way over to his desk, stepping over the tangled piles of clothes and hats and scarves and other random accessories that littered the floor – his half of the floor anyway. As usual, his room-mate MJ's side was immaculate. Andre itched to be able to invade MJ's floor and wall space – their bareness seemed such a waste, especially when there were so many fun things he could be filling them with. He flung the harem pants on to the floor and retrieved the piece of paper detailing his History assignment. Andre really didn't see the point in history. It was over and done with; been there, done that. All Andre was interested in was the future. Because the future was the place where your dreams came true. He didn't have time to be harking back to some pre-historic king who liked killing his wives or whatever. How was that ever going to help him achieve his dance and fashion dreams?

He returned to his laptop to make a start on the assignment but couldn't resist having one more check of Spotted first. His heart sank. Three people had liked the nappy comment! What the hell? His blog wasn't supposed to be for people to come and have a laugh. It wasn't a comedy site. It was supposed to be for serious fashionistas. He bet other fashion sites didn't get this kind of disrespect. He clicked on to one of his favourite fashion blogs and started randomly checking the comments. They were all positive. There wasn't a single joke. He clicked on to another fashion site, one that had 475,820 subscribers. Andre sighed. How was he ever going to get that many people to subscribe to Spotted? He clicked back on to his own blog. He had 357 subscribers. And instead of growing, that list had shrunk by two today. All because of those stupid harem pants. He went over to the offending pile of trousers and grabbed some scissors from his desk. He started slashing at one of the pairs. They were bright green with silver sequins sewn into the waistband. Tilly had found them in a charity shop. At the time, the trousers had passed the tingle test – anything they featured on the blog had to make their skin tingle with excitement – but it turned out that the tingle test itself had failed. Andre started ripping the harem pants apart with his hands. 'Die, stupid trousers, die! What was I even thinking?'

The door to the dorm room opened and MJ walked in, followed closely by Tilly.

'What the hell are you doing?' she asked, staring at him in shock.

'I'm killing the harem pants,' Andre replied, with yet another satisfying rip.

'You can't kill an inanimate object,' MJ said drily, dumping his overnight bag on his bed.

'Just watch me,' Andre responded.

'But why?' Tilly asked, playing with the ends of her peacock green hair, the way she always did when she was confused or stressed.

'Because they're a laughing stock,' Andre replied, sinking down on to his bed. 'Have you seen the comment, Tillz?'

'What comment?' She came and sat down beside him.

'Nice eye-liner by the way,' Andre added. Even in the grips of a crisis he was still able to acknowledge a cosmetics win when he saw one.

'Thank you. Now what on earth's going on?'

Andre passed her the laptop. 'Look. The harem-pant post has got way fewer likes than normal, plus one snidey comment and two people have unsubscribed. It's a catastrophe!'

'Hmm, tell that to the people of Syria,' MJ remarked.

'Not helpful, MJ, not helpful at all,' Andre muttered.

Tilly looked at the screen and started to laugh.

'What's so funny?' Andre stared at her.

'The comment.'

'I'm sorry?'

'Well, it is kind of true. There could be a giant nappy under there.'

'Great!' Andre sighed. Tilly was supposed to be his second-in-command at Spotted. She was supposed to be on his side. Not on the side of some smarty-harem-pants-hater who thought @fashattack was a good profile name. *Geez!*

'Hey, lighten up, Dre,' Tilly said, nudging him gently in the ribs. 'It's only a joke.'

'What does that say?' Andre said, pointing to the banner of the blog.

'*Spotted . . . unleash your inner fashionista,*' Tilly said, reading from the screen.

'Exactly. Does it say, unleash your inner comedian?'

'No.'

'And does it say, please feel free to leave your lame jokes in the comments?'

'No but –'

'There can be no buts,' Andre interrupted. 'And there should be no jokes. Fashion is a serious business.'

'Hmm, tell that to whoever invented platform heels,' MJ remarked.

'Er, still not helping, MJ!' Andre retorted.

'OK, I'm not sure what happened to bring about this crisis, Dre, but I do know what will fix it.' Tilly stood up and held out her hands to him.

Andre looked at her blankly. 'What?'

'Dancing, of course. Let's hit the Stable Studio. Do a little free-styling. What do you say, MJ?'

MJ got to his feet. 'Yep, sounds good to me.'

They both looked at Andre. Andre frowned. If he went to the studio they'd probably expect him to come up with some kind of new routine for Il Bello and he just couldn't deal with that right now. He felt like an iPhone that had run out of storage space. He needed an urgent reboot.

'I can't,' he said. 'I have homework to do.'

'What?' Tilly's mouth dropped open. 'But, Dre, you never say no to dance.'

'Yeah well. I used to have three hundred and fifty-nine followers on my blog.'

'What's that got to do with it?'

'Things change, Tillz, and so do people.'

Tilly looked dejected. 'Wow. OK then.' She turned to MJ. 'Shall we see if Raf's about?'

'Good plan,' MJ replied.

Tilly took hold of Andre's arm. 'You know where we are if you change your mind.'

Andre nodded.

'Take it easy, Dre. You're just having a bad day.'

Tilly gave him a quick hug then headed for the door.

As Andre watched them leave he felt a bitter-sweet mix of sorrow and relief. He couldn't believe he was turning down the chance to dance but at least it eased the pressure a fraction. He needed to get that History assignment done. But first, he'd have another check of his blog.

CHAPTER TWO

As his History teacher, Mr Benson, droned on about Queen Elizabeth I Andre's head started feeling warm and fuzzy with tiredness. He'd hardly slept at all last night – he'd been too preoccupied with Spotted and trying to figure out ways to get more subscribers. Things that had seemed like a great idea at three in the morning – like creating three hundred thousand different online personas to follow Spotted – now seemed pretty insane. But what could he do?

'Queen Elizabeth I was just two years old when her mother, Anne Boleyn, was beheaded,' Mr Benson said as he strolled around the class.

Next to Andre, Raf whistled through his teeth.

But Andre really couldn't see what the big deal was. That's how things were back then – queens got beheaded. It was almost part of the job description. At least they never had to deal with the internet. At least they never had to worry about things like subscribers and likes and hashtags . . . Hashtags! Andre's heavy eyelids jolted open. Maybe that was the answer. Maybe he had to up his hashtag game.

'Eleven days after Anne Boleyn's execution, Henry VIII married Jane Seymour,' Mr Benson continued.

Andre's eyelids drooped back down again. It was as if his entire upper body was feeling a huge gravitational pull towards the desk. Maybe if he just rested his forehead on it for a while, had a think about some killer hashtags . . . He closed his eyes and let his head sink desk-wards. Then he felt a sharp dig in his ribs.

'Hashtag harem!' he yelped. 'Ow!' He frowned at Raf. 'Why'd you do that?'

'You were falling asleep, bro,' Raf hissed.

'Hashtag harem indeed,' Mr Benson said with a grin and laughter rippled through the class.

'What?' Andre stared at him blankly. Oh shoot, had he actually said that out loud?

'Henry VIII and all his wives,' Mr Benson said. 'His Tudor harem.'

'Oh . . . right.' Andre sat up straight, trying desperately to wake himself up.

Mr Benson carried on chatting about Queen Elizabeth and Andre took a deep breath. It was so frustrating being in this dumb class having to learn about people that meant absolutely nothing to him. It was such a waste of time. No wonder he was almost falling asleep. He could be doing something far more useful – like coming up with a list of hashtags or brainstorming fresh new blog ideas. He thought of his phone in the pocket of his jacket. The urge to check it was almost as strong as the urge to sleep. While he'd been sitting through blah-blah-beheading-blah he could have got more notifications from Spotted. Other people might have commented. Other people might have liked the stupid nappy comment. These were the things he needed to know – not where the young Elizabeth had lived while her psycho dad was out killing wives.

Finally the bell rang for end of period. Andre leaped to his feet.

'Easy, bro,' Raf said with one of his dazzling grins.

'I need to check something,' Andre said, heading for the door. 'I'll see you in tap.' He raced to the toilets, locked himself inside a cubicle and checked his phone. He had a new email. His heart quickened. What if it was a notification from the blog? But it was just a message from a fashion newsletter he subscribed to. He clicked it open. The layout of the newsletter was so slick. He clicked on their Instagram link at the bottom of the page. They had over one million subscribers. How was that even possible? He unlocked the cubicle door and went over to one of the sinks. He splashed some water on his face and stared at his reflection. He'd give anything to have that kind of following. When you had that kind of following you no longer had to worry any more – you knew that you'd made it. What if he never got where he wanted to be? What if the online empire he dreamed of building never materialized? What if all he ever achieved was an online cul-de-sac? He couldn't bear the thought.

The bell rang again, signalling the start of the next period. Shoot! His tap class was over in the new building. He was going to be late. Mrs Jones was not going to be pleased.

Mrs Jones *wasn't* pleased. As Andre raced into the studio, clutching his tap shoes in his hands she rapped on the polished wood floor with her cane.

'And what time do you call this?' she asked.

'Time you took pity on a poor, defenceless soul who just got trapped inside a toilet cubicle?' Andre looked at her pleadingly. He wasn't sure how convincing an excuse getting trapped inside a toilet cubicle was but it was the best he could do under the circumstances.

'You got trapped inside a toilet cubicle?'

Mrs Jones looked at him sternly while the rest of the class grinned.

'Yes. It was terrible. I wasn't sure I'd ever be rescued. Now I know how Anne Boleyn felt right before her execution.'

'You're likening getting trapped inside a toilet with being beheaded?' Mrs Jones raised her eyebrows so high they practically met her snowy white hairline. The other students started to snigger.

'Don't laugh!' Andre retorted. 'The panic was real!'

'OK. I've heard enough,' Mrs Jones said. Although she was still frowning Andre could see that her gaze had softened a fraction. 'Get your shoes on and take your place.'

'Why do you always have to be such a drama queen?' Cassandra whispered as Andre put his shoes on.

'Same reason you have to be such an ice queen, I guess,' Andre retorted. 'I was born this way.' Andre had no time for Cassandra. Ever since they'd started at WEDA she'd gone out of her way to make Billie and Tilly's lives hell. As far as Andre was concerned, if you messed with a member of Il Bello, you messed with him.

'OK, everyone, places, please,' Mrs Jones called. 'Let's begin with a single file line for our tap cannons, starting with a stamp slide into a spank heel step flap ball change. Listen to each other to stay in time or you will end up sounding like a herd of buffalo stampeding. We need to make beautiful rhythms, not a mush of melodies.'

As the music started Andre focused hard on waiting for his turn to step in beat and stay in rhythm but his entire body ached with tiredness and his limbs felt as limp as a rag doll's. Each time the cannon came to him he was a split second behind the beat and pulled everyone else out of rhythm. *Come on, focus*, he told himself but it was no good. It was as if his brain and his feet were living separate lives.

'Aaargh!' he exclaimed, as Mrs Jones tapped

her cane on the floor to get them to stop.

'So, a herd of buffalo it is. Is everything OK, Andre?' she asked.

The whole class turned to stare at him.

'I do hope you're not still traumatized by your toilet ordeal.'

As the others giggled Andre felt an unfamiliar warmth in his cheeks. 'No. It's not that, it's . . .'

'What?' Mrs Jones asked.

Andre saw Cassandra smirking. Great.

'I just don't like it when I don't bring my A game,' he muttered.

'Yes.' Mrs Jones nodded. 'And there's only one answer to that – wake up and work harder!' She rapped her cane on the floor. 'OK, everyone, let's take it from the top.'

As the cannon started again Raf placed his hand on Andre's shoulder. 'Go easy on yourself, bro. We all have those days.'

Andre nodded. But Raf didn't understand. This wasn't just one of those days. He had great big, clumsy buffalo feet *and* a blogging empire crumbling around him.

At lunchtime Andre made his way to the Stable Studio. Normally, these lunchtime sessions with Il Bello were the highlight of his school day but today, as he made his way along the winding path through the trees at the back of the old building, he felt a creeping sense of dread. The others would all be expecting him to have come up with some new choreography ideas and what with Harem-Pant Hell, History Homework Hell and Buffalo Herd Hell he just hadn't had a chance to think of anything.

He let himself into the stable. The others were there already, gathered together at the far end. Hazy gold pools of sunlight poured through the skylights on to the shiny wooden floor. It was hard to imagine that at the beginning of the school year, when Andre had first claimed the building for his street crew HQ, it had been a run-down old stable. So much had changed since then. Now, not only was the stable converted into a state-of-the-art studio but, thanks to Il Bello, street dance was on the curriculum at WEDA. He should feel proud of this but instead it only added to his feeling of exhaustion. He looked at Tilly's graffiti mural on the wall – the three street-style bumble bees that symbolized the Il Bello three Bs ethos: *Be fearless. Be authentic. Be you.* No one had warned him it could be so stressful being authentic.

'Dre!' Billie exclaimed, running over to greet him. Her blond hair was swept back into a ponytail and she was wearing a vintage AC/DC rock-band tee over ripped leggings. Normally Andre would have commented on her fashion win but today he was so tired he couldn't summon the energy to gush.

'Hey, Bill,' he said.

'We were just wondering what music to play. What do you reckon?' Billie looked at him hopefully. It was a look he was used to. And he'd always liked that they valued his opinion so much but today it made him irritable. Why should everything always be down to him?

'I don't know,' he said, making his way over to the others.

'Oh, come on, Dre – you always know,' Billie replied.

The others started nodding. It made him want to scream.

'No. No I don't. My playlists are played out and anyway, why do we even need to rehearse? It's not as if we have a show coming up.'

Billie's face fell. 'You don't want to dance?'

Tilly came over and placed her hand on Andre's forehead. 'Have you got a fever or something? That's the second time in two days you've said you don't want to dance.'

'I'm just having a down day, don't make such a big deal of it. I can't carry you all the time . . .' Andre stopped, mortified at what had just come out of his mouth. This wasn't how he was. He had to get out of there.

'Actually, you know what, maybe I am coming down with something.' Andre picked up his bag.

'You guys go ahead without me. I need some fresh air.'

He made his way back outside, feeling drained and embarrassed. What the hell was wrong with him, talking to the others like that?

He heard footsteps running up behind him and turned to see Tilly.

'Oh, Dre, what's wrong?' she said, grabbing him in a hug.

'Nothing – I . . .' Andre leaned his head on her shoulder. It felt so nice. He was so sleepy. Maybe he should tell her everything. But he was supposed to be the strong one – the leader of Il Bello. It was bad enough that he'd just had a mini-meltdown. 'I've been a bit stressed about Spotted, that's all.'

'But why?' Tilly took a step back and stared at him. 'Spotted is doing great.'

'I wish we had more subscribers.'

'We will. It takes time.' Tilly smiled. 'I know. Let's go out tomorrow – spot some new looks. That's guaranteed to make you feel better.'

Andre nodded but inside he wasn't so sure. In his current mood, even the thought of his favourite pastime fashion-spotting left him feeling flat.

CHAPTER THREE

'Oh my God! This town is so dull it makes watching paint dry seem like a thriller.' Andre looked around the shopping precinct and gave a dramatic sigh.

'Chill, Dre,' Tilly replied. 'It's good that it's boring.'

'Oh yeah?' Andre stared at her. 'Why's that?'

Tilly adjusted her peaked cap. 'Because it means that when we do finally spot a great look it'll really stand out.'

Andre leaned over the wall of the gallery to look down to the floor below. The precinct was full of frazzled-looking parents pushing buggies, and scruffy school kids. How were they ever going to find a good look here? It was like a blazer-wearing, toddler-wrangling zombie apocalypse. They should have gone into London instead but of course he didn't have enough time. He had yet another History assignment that was due in tomorrow.

'What about that guy?' Tilly said, pointing to a boy of about sixteen who was leaning against the wall beneath a sign for the public toilets.

'Are you serious? He's wearing a McDonald's uniform!'

'I know. But maybe we could do a post on fast-food fashion?'

Andre cocked his head as if he was listening hard to something. 'Wait, what's that I hear?'

Tilly frowned. 'What?'

'The sound of the bottom of the barrel being scraped. Fast-food fashion? What the hell? Fast food is the enemy of the animals, Tillz, and nothing can help that tragic uniform.'

'It could be ironic,' Tilly said lamely. 'Or we could do a top tips kind of thing. Like, how to stop your work uniform looking so naff.'

'Do you think *Vogue* would ever do a fast-food fashion feature?'

'No but . . .'

'But what?'

'Spotted isn't *Vogue*.'

Andre's heart sank. What was Tilly trying to say? They weren't *Vogue* . . . and they never would be? He looked back at the McDonald's guy and his stomach rumbled. He could murder a burger right now. 'Oy vey!' he muttered under his breath.

Tilly hooked her arm in his. 'What is it? What's up, Dre?'

'Nothing. I'm just hangry.' Andre tore his eyes away from the McDonald's guy. He was not going to give up on being vegan, no way. He wasn't a heartless animal murderer like his dad. He was better than that.

'What's hangry?' Tilly asked.

'It's when you're so hungry you become angry and right now I am at boiling point, *toooot!*'

'Why don't we go and get something to eat then?'

Tilly said, her face brightening. 'You never know, we might spot someone cool in the sandwich bar.'

'Yeah, and bacon sandwiches might fly.' Andre sighed. 'OK then, let's go cure this hanger.'

Once they'd got their sandwiches – salmon for Tilly and humous and vegetables for Andre – Tilly took off her cap and stared at him.

'What is it, Dre? You haven't been your normal self at all lately. We're all worried about you.'

'All?' Andre frowned.

'Yes, all of Il Bello.'

Andre felt a warm glow inside as he imagined the street crew huddled together talking about him, their faces full of concern. *It's killing me that he's so down,* he imagined Billie saying. *Andre is our everything, I don't know what we'd do without him.* The warm glow faded. He didn't want to be their everything. It was too much pressure.

'What's going on?' Tilly continued.

'Nothing. It's just . . . I've been worried

about Spotted . . . about losing subscribers. That harem-pant post didn't get nearly as many likes as our previous posts. I'm worried I'm losing my touch.'

'You're not losing your touch! Oh my God, Dre, you're the most fabulous person I've ever met.'

'Really?' Andre searched her face for any evidence she was lying but Tilly's eyes were wide and deadly serious.

'Of course. You're FETCH with a capital everything, remember.'

Andre nodded. 'It's true.'

Tilly leaned forward, her face lighting up. 'I've got it!'

'Got what?'

'Who we need to feature on our next post.'

Andre looked around the sandwich bar behind him. A middle-aged guy wearing a greasy anorak and sporting the lamest comb-over was sitting by the door stuffing some kind of pie into his face. Gravy was trickling down his chin.

'You've got to be kidding? You want to do a feature on pie-face chic?'

'What?' Tilly looked at the guy. 'No! Not him – you.'

'Me?'

'Yes. We should feature you as the founder of Spotted.'

'But there's already something on me on the About page.'

'Yes, but it isn't a proper feature.' Tilly was beaming now. 'Go on, it would be great. We can do a proper photo shoot – in the Stable Studio. I could get some epic shots of you in there.'

'Do you really think it would be a good idea?' Andre could tell from her face that she did but he wanted to hear her say it again. He could never have too much of hearing people say he was fabulous.

'Yes! You're everything that Spotted is about . . . and your look is always on point.'

'What about my hair – don't forget my hair,' Andre prompted.

Tilly grinned. 'Yes, Dre – you have the fetchest hair in the entire universe.'

Andre grinned back at her. Tilly was right. It would be great to feature himself on Spotted. It was a chance to publish a new post and make himself feel better all in one go.

'OK, you're on,' he said.

'Awesome!' Tilly replied.

When they got back to WEDA Tilly went straight to the Stable Studio to sort out the lights and camera for the shoot and Andre headed for his dorm room to pick an outfit. Thankfully, MJ wasn't there. Andre loved his straight-talking room-mate but sometimes – like when Andre was trying to figure out what to wear – his dry commentary could get a little annoying.

'OK, let's create a fashion masterpiece!' Andre declared, flinging his wardrobe door open. 'Oh . . .' His wardrobe was practically empty. He turned and looked around his side of the room. His wardrobe was practically empty because almost all of his clothes seemed to be draped over every piece of furniture and most of the floor. Andre started making three separate heaps on the floor – YES, NO and MAYBE. When he came across his favourite pair of harem pants he shuddered and was about to fling them on the NO pile when he had a thought. He'd always loved those trousers. He'd got them from his favourite flea market in New York. Why should he let some stupid joker's comments put him off his beloved trousers? What if he wore them for the shoot? Reclaimed the harem pant – made them fashion forward again. Andre's skin started to tingle. He was a young man on a mission. He put the harem pants in the YES pile.

Almost a whole hour later – and after several texts from Tilly along the lines of 'Where the hell are you?' – Andre had completed his look. As well as the harem pants he was wearing Docs with the laces undone, his favourite vintage Adidas shirt and a couple of gold chains, and his fingers were adorned in gold rings.

'And now for the finishing touch,' he said to his reflection in the wardrobe mirror before fetching his black mascara from his desk drawer. He added a touch to his eyelashes for extra pop. Whenever anyone asked if he was wearing make-up he always fluttered his eyelashes and said, 'Who, me? Darling, I was born this way!' He stepped back and admired his finished look.

'On. Point,' he murmured with a grin.

His phone started ringing, rudely interrupting his self-admiration party. He didn't have to look at the caller ID to know it would be Tilly. 'OK, OK, I'm coming already.' He grabbed his room keys and headed for the door.

Down in the Stable Studio Tilly had set up a couple of lights in front of her graffiti mural and she had her favourite Twenty One Pilots track playing.

'At last!' she said as Andre came in.

'I'm sorry but a true diva cannot hurry his craft,'

Andre said, coming to stand in front of her. 'What do you reckon?'

'You look amazing!' Tilly grinned. 'I love those harem pants on you.'

'You do?' Andre felt a burst of relief.

'Yeah. We should have featured you in the post last week. I bet you'd have got hundreds of likes.'

Andre felt some of the tension he'd been carrying for the past few days ease a little. Maybe last week's dip in likes was just a blip. Now was his chance to prove it.

'OK, what do you want me to do?'

For the next hour Tilly got Andre to stand in a series of poses. She also got some great action shots of him doing some big dance jumps. 'We can capture your two loves – dance and fashion – in action,' she explained. 'We can show how movement can capture the beauty of the fabric and just how awesome harem pants are for dance. I mean, you can dress them up or down, lounge around, dance in them and do amazing jumps.

They are the forever trouser. People need to get with the times already!'

Once they'd got a selection of shots they were happy with they went back to Andre's room to write a post to go with them.

'How about I interview you?' Tilly said, sitting cross-legged on Andre's bed. 'I can record your answers on my phone and then you can type them up.'

'Sounds good to me.' Actually it sounded *great* to Andre. He could pretend he was being interviewed by Anna Wintour for *Vogue*. He leaned back on his pillows as Tilly switched on the voice recorder on her phone.

'So, Andre, who is your greatest inspiration?' Tilly asked.

'Vivienne Westwood,' Andre replied instantly, closing his eyes and imagining he was in *Vogue*'s office in New York.

'And why is that?'

'Well, Anna, it's –'

'Anna?' Tilly interrupted.

Andre opened his eyes and frowned at her. 'What?'

'Why did you call me Anna?'

'I didn't.'

'Yes you did.'

'Look, are we going to do this interview or what?'

Tilly sighed. 'OK. Carry on.'

'Vivienne Westwood is my inspiration. She never tries to fit into a mould. She always does her own thing. And she's eco-conscious, vegetarian and fearless. I love her quote: "Popular culture is a contradiction in terms. If it's popular, it's not culture." That's what I try to create with my own look – something new and fresh. Fashion shouldn't be about copying everyone else.'

'So true.' Tilly nodded. 'Could you tell us some more about you and who you aspire to be?'

'Sure. I aspire to be fearless and authentic at all times. I also care deeply for the planet we live on – and animals. I recently became vegan and I never want to go near meat again. Just the thought of it makes me sick.' The image of a burger popped into Andre's mind and his mouth started to water.

'That's great.' Tilly smiled. 'Now, as well as running this blog and being a full-time fashionista you're currently a student at the World Elite Dance Academy. Could you tell us what dance means to you?'

'Dance means everything to me,' Andre replied. 'Dance is where I feel most free to be me. Like, when I'm dancing – especially when I'm on stage – nothing else matters. It's the only place I'm able to totally let go and allow the music and my mood to take over. Apart from the end-of-season sale rail.'

Tilly laughed. 'Word. And finally, what are your dreams for the future?'

'I'd like to make it as a world-class dancer and build this blog into an online fashion empire.' As Andre said the words he felt a nervous twinge, the return of the doubt and anxiety he'd been feeling. What if he didn't make it? What if he didn't achieve those dreams? He pushed his doubts away and smiled at Tilly.

'That was great,' she said. 'It's going to make an awesome post.'

'You think?'

'I know.'

'OK. Well, I'd better get typing it up.' Andre looked at the clock. It was getting late. If he worked on the post tonight he wouldn't have time to do his History assignment. He shrugged to himself. The blog post was more important than his History class. It was about his future, not the past. And right now, his future – and making sure it was an awesome one – was all that counted.

CHAPTER FOUR

When he finally got to bed that night Andre found it really hard to sleep. He'd spent so long staring at the computer screen, trying to get the layout of the blog post just right and playing around with different fonts for the text, his head was buzzing. Every time he felt like he was about to drop off he'd wonder what kind of response the post was getting and his eyes would flick open. Somehow he managed to resist the urge to check his phone and he eventually fell asleep. But he dropped straight into the nightmare from hell.

In it, Mrs Jones was giving a WEDA assembly and he'd been called to the stage.

'We'd like you to give a presentation on your

blog,' Mrs Jones told him, pointing to a laptop that had been set up on the lectern. 'Please could you show the students some of your latest posts?'

Andre clicked on the Spotted page and it was projected on to a large screen behind him. Gasps rang out throughout the hall, causing Andre to beam with pride. But then the gasps changed to laughter. He turned to look at the screen . . . and saw that the blog post featured pictures of him wearing a giant nappy. 'OMG!' He gasped, trying to flick to another page. But no matter how hard he clicked on the trackpad the screen wouldn't change. Then he noticed something else that made his blood run cold. Spotted had no subscribers. The figure on the right-hand column of the page was a big fat zero. 'No!' Andre cried out loud, waking himself up.

He sat bolt upright in bed, breathing heavily. *It's OK, it was just a dream*, he told himself as he rubbed the sleep from his eyes. But *was* it a dream? Or was it a premonition? He got out of bed and tiptoed over to his wardrobe, being careful not to wake MJ. It was still the middle of the night. He rooted around in his pile of shoes until he found his phone inside a Doc Marten, where he'd stuffed it before he went to bed to stop himself from checking it.

He crept back to his bed and turned his phone on, his heart skipping a beat at the sight of the blue notification light. He had eleven new emails – most of them comment notifications from Spotted. Nervously, he clicked on his blog. Thankfully, he was still fully dressed in perfect dance fashion in the photos on his post. And even more thankfully, the number of subscribers was exactly the same and hadn't crashed to zero. The post had also got way more likes than the previous one had by this point so that was a good sign. But what about the comments? What if @fashattack had made another joke? He scrolled down to check them. The first three were all great . . .

@anna_175: Love it!
@bootboy: sick look, bruh!

@jamieluvsjosh: your hair is on fleek J

But then Andre read a comment that made his stomach flip . . .

@snarkerella: oh yawn – yet another Vivienne Westwood wannabe – and not a very good one either. And what's up with his eyebrows?

Andre instinctively raised a hand to his forehead. What *was* up with his eyebrows? He'd spent ages plucking them to perfection. What did @snarkerella mean? And what was with the Vivienne Westwood dig? Was that how he looked? Like some kind of lame-ass wannabe?

Andre got out of bed and started pacing up and down MJ's side of the room – there was no space to pace on his side due to the clothes mountains. He'd always prided himself on being original – but maybe even being original wasn't original any more because other people, like Vivienne Westwood, had been original before him. *Aaaargh!*

'What are you doing?' MJ muttered from beneath his duvet, his voice groggy from sleep.

'Pacing,' Andre replied.

'Racing?' MJ asked.

'No! Pacing . . . like, up and down. Like people do when they're stressed.'

Through the darkness Andre could just make out MJ shifting into a seated position.

'Are you stressed?'

'Yes.'

'Why?'

'Because I've just been trolled.'

'What, while you were asleep?' MJ turned on his bedside lamp and frowned at him.

'Yes – online. On Spotted.' Andre continued pacing. He never should have featured himself on the blog, especially so soon after Harem-Pant Hell. It was asking for trouble.

'Oh. What did they say?'

'What did who say?'

'The troll.'

'They called me a Vivienne Westwood wannabe – and not a very good one either. And they made fun of my eyebrows.'

'Your eyebrows?' MJ stared at Andre, clearly now wide awake. 'But your eyebrows are –'

'My pride and joy. Yes, I know,' Andre interrupted. 'But it turns out I was wrong. Turns out they're hideous.'

'Is that what the troll said? That they're hideous.'

'Not exactly – but that's what they meant. I can tell. Look.' Andre handed MJ his phone and waited for a gasp of outrage.

'But it isn't true,' MJ said, matter-of-factly.

'What isn't?'

'What they say. So why are you letting it bother you?'

'I – uh . . .'

'Just go back to sleep. This person's an idiot. They don't even know you.' MJ turned off his lamp and lay back down.

Andre stared into the darkness. @snarkerella might not know him but the blog post *was* him. The words and the photos, they were all Andre expressing his authentic self – and his eyebrows – and he'd been mocked for it. There was no way he'd be able to go back to sleep now.

The next morning in History, Andre hunched down in his chair at the back of the class, trying to make himself invisible. Maybe if he kept a super-low profile Mr Benson wouldn't notice him and he wouldn't ask for the homework he hadn't done. As Mr Benson got closer, Andre slid further and further down in his seat until his nose was practically level with the desk.

'Andre?' Mr Benson said.

Damn! 'Yes, Mr Benson?'

'Is everything OK?'

'Yes, sir. Why?'

'Perhaps you'd like to adopt a more vertical position.'

'Sorry, Mr Benson.' Andre shuffled back upright.

'And hand me your homework.'

'Ah, I was wondering if you were going to ask me that.'

Mr Benson put his hand on his hip disappointedly. 'Really? I don't think it's any great surprise, Andre. Given that I just announced to the entire class that I was coming round collecting your papers.'

The rest of the class started laughing. Great, that was all he needed – a teacher who thought he was a comedian.

'I'm afraid I don't have my paper,' Andre said, staring straight ahead.

'And why is that?'

Andre tried to pull an elaborate lie from thin air but he couldn't think of anything – he was too tired. 'I . . . er . . . something more important came up.'

A hushed silence fell in the room as everyone turned to see how Mr Benson would respond.

'Something more important than the Spanish Armada?'

'Yes.'

Mr Benson put down the pile of homework he'd collected and folded his arms. 'Well, don't keep us all in suspense. What was more important than one of England's finest naval victories?'

'My blog,' Andre muttered.

Cassandra gave a sarcastic laugh.

'Your blog,' Mr Benson said, with a look of disbelief.

'Yes.' Andre took a deep breath. Sometimes the best defence was to go on the attack. 'I don't mean to be rude, Mr Benson, but history, well, it's kind of irrelevant. I mean, I'm sure it's interesting to old people but for us . . .' He looked around the class, desperate for someone to back him up but everyone was staring at him like they were watching a car crash. 'For us younger people it doesn't mean a thing. For us it's all about the future. And I needed to write a blog post last night because my blog is my future. If I'm ever going to have an online empire I need to start now.'

'An online empire?' Mr Benson echoed.

'Yes.'

Mr Benson stood upright, his face taut with anger. 'Well, I'm sorry you feel that way, Andre. And as my lessons are clearly so boring and irrelevant to you I suggest you take your things and go straight to Miss Murphy's office.'

'What? But –'

'Now!' Mr Benson barked.

Andre stumbled to his feet. Great, that was all he needed – a telling off from his mum. This day was going from bad to worse.

'What do you mean, Mr Benson's having a midlife crisis?' Miss Murphy stared at Andre across her desk.

'He has to be,' Andre said. 'The way he overreacted to what I said in class.'

Miss Murphy leaned back in her chair, still treating him to one of her steely stares. 'And what exactly did you say in class?'

'I just told him why I wasn't able to get my

homework done and he freaked out.'

'Why weren't you able to get your homework done?'

'I was working on a blog post for Spotted. I had to get it done, Mum. And I tried to explain to Mr Benson about History being irrelevant but he didn't want to know.'

Miss Murphy sat bolt upright. 'You told Mr Benson that History was irrelevant?'

'Yes. Well it is.'

'Oh, Andre. What's gotten into you?'

'What do you mean? It *is* irrelevant to people my age. We need to be focusing on the future – on building our . . . on our goals.'

Miss Murphy sighed. 'History isn't irrelevant at all. I can't believe you were so rude to Mr Benson.'

It was Andre's turn to stare at his mum. He couldn't believe she was being such a traitor! This was how Anne Boleyn must have felt when her psycho husband yelled, 'Off with her head!' It was so unfair.

Miss Murphy got to her feet. 'And Mrs Jones told me that you were struggling in your tap class the other day.'

Great, another traitor.

'I was just having an off day, that's all.'

'Are you sure?' Miss Murphy gave him one of her x-ray stares that had the power to see right through his skull and read his mind.

'Yes.'

'Hmm, well in that case I want you to write a letter of apology to Mr Benson and –'

'A letter!'

'Yes.'

'What, you mean, on paper?'

Miss Murphy started rummaging in her desk drawer. 'Yes. And with a pen – to make it more personal.'

'But no one writes letters any more!'

'I want you to write him a letter, Andre.' Miss Murphy took some paper from her desk drawer and handed it to him. 'Right here, right now.

You can take it to him at the end of the period.'

Andre sighed and sat down. Just when he thought things couldn't get any worse, he ended up in some kind of historical hell. He wouldn't be surprised if his mum got a quill and a pot of ink out and made him write it in that – or maybe she'd prefer he write in his own blood.

She handed him a biro. 'Go on, get started.'

Andre did the mother of all sighs and began to write.

Once he'd delivered his grovelling letter of apology – it had taken three attempts to get it right, apparently using phrases like '*I most humbly apologise for my crimes against History*' sounded like he was being insincere – Andre made his way to the Stable Studio. He needed to see Il Bello. He needed to see some people who actually belonged in the twenty-first century.

'Hey, Dre,' Billie called as he let himself into the studio. 'Raf was just telling us what happened in your History lesson.'

'Don't remind me.' Andre grimaced. 'I've come here to try to forget about it all.'

'Are you OK?' Tilly asked. 'MJ told us about the comment on your new blog post too. You know it's all rubbish, right? You aren't a wannabe anything, you're unique.'

'Yeah, and you have eyebrows to die for,' Billie added.

'Seriously?' Andre looked around at them.

'Absolutely,' Raf said. 'Although I don't think I'd actually, like, die for your eyebrows but you know, they are pretty cool.'

'Thank you.' Andre put his bag on the floor and took off his jacket. 'Could we – could we just dance?'

'Of course!' Tilly exclaimed and MJ picked a track on his phone.

'Human' by Rag'n'Bone Man started playing. Andre stretched his arms up over his head and closed his eyes. He let the beat work its way inside of his body and slowly started to groove in time. As the words sank deep inside his mind they ignited a fire inside of him. The song built and his movements became more forceful. All of the stress and hurt that had been swilling around inside of him started transforming into a white-hot rage as he hit hard, popping to the beats of the song. His emotion was more powerful than ever before. He finally felt some release. @snarkerella had no right to make snide comments about him. No one did. He'd show them that he wasn't just a wannabe. He'd show them that he had eyebrows to die for. He arched and spun and bent and whipped his body to the rhythm until the track came to an end.

'Wow, Dre, you were slaying it just then,' Tilly said, gaping.

Andre bent over to catch his breath. He'd been so lost in his thoughts and the dance he'd forgotten the others were even there.

'Yeah, bro, sick moves,' Raf said, patting him on the back.

'Thanks.' Andre picked up his jacket and bag.

'Where are you going?' Billie asked.

'There's something I need to do,' Andre replied. 'I'll see you guys later.' He hurried from the Stable Studio and made his way back to his room. He logged on to Spotted and hit reply to @snarkerella's comment.

> oh yawn – yet another wise-cracking
> wannabe, and not a very good one either.
> And what's up with your personality? Lose it
> on the way to UGLY TOWN?

He hit the reply button and felt a sharp stab of satisfaction as he saw his words on the screen. That would show @snarkerella not to mess with him. But he couldn't help noticing that his relief was tinged with doubt. Was it right to have stooped to their level? Should he have just left it? But if he'd left it it meant that they had won. And they couldn't win. This was his blog, his life and no one was going to mess with it.

CHAPTER FIVE

All stayed quiet on the Spotted front for the rest of the day, until last period. Andre knew because he was checking every half-second, wondering if @snarkerella would reply. When Andre checked his phone again on the way to his tap class he saw that he had seventeen new comment notifications. His heart plummeted as he dived inside a store cupboard to check them. They were all from @snarkerella. The first one was a reply to his reply.

@snarkerella: 'ugly town'???!!! Pot calling kettle black much? You need to take a look in the mirror. And the fact that you mainly used my own words in your reply shows how unoriginal you are

Andre felt sick. He thought he'd been clever, turning @snarkerella's words back on them but all he'd done was give them more ammunition. He scrolled down the screen to the rest of the comments. @snarkerella had gone back over old posts leaving snarky comments galore. Then Andre saw one that made his blood boil. They'd made a dig about Tilly's flamingo hat. He deleted the comment instantly, hoping Tilly wouldn't have seen it. Then he deleted all the other comments. The bell rang for the start of class. Damn! He was going to be late for Mrs Jones again. Andre stuffed the phone in his pocket. As soon as class was over he'd change the security settings on Spotted and figure out how to block @snarkerella. He raced over to the new building and burst into the studio. The others were already dancing.

'Sorry I'm late,' he said, gasping. 'I – uh –'

'Don't tell me – you got trapped in the toilet again,' Mrs Jones said with a frown.

Cassandra sniggered.

'No – I – it was a store room,' Andre replied lamely.

'You got trapped in a store room?' Mrs Jones glared at him.

'No . . . I didn't get trapped this time I –'

'This is the second time this week you've been late, Andre. It really isn't acceptable.'

'I know. I'm sorry. It won't happen again.'

'You're right. It won't. Not if you want to stay in this class.'

Andre pulled on his tap shoes, his heart pounding. He couldn't believe she was threatening to drop him from her class. He couldn't fail tap. He'd never failed anything.

Mrs Jones rapped her cane on the floor. 'All right, everyone, let's warm up, starting with eight taps, front, side and back, then moving to flaps and shuffles. Keep your ankles nice and loose with a slight bend at the knee to get full and ample sound.' She started the music and the class followed her.

For the rest of the class all Andre could think

about was @snarkerella. What if they'd posted more horrible comments? What if other people had seen them? What if Spotted became a train wreck of a blog – somewhere people came purely to take a look at the trolling like some kind of sick spectator sport?

'Andre, please!' Mrs Jones yelled at one point, when he completely mistimed a step and crashed into Raf. 'Focus!'

Andre fought the urge to yell back. None of the teachers here understood what he was going through. They had no idea what it was like to try to build an online empire; they were all obsessed with the olden days when people did lame-ass things like write letters by hand.

After what felt like one hundred years, the bell rang for the end of period. Andre raced over to his bag and pulled out his phone. The notification light was blinking. Seven new comments had been posted on Spotted. But before he could check them he heard the sharp rap of Mrs Jones's cane right behind him.

'Andre Murphy!' she yelled.

The rest of the class fell silent. Fantastic, he was about to be made a total idiot of again. He turned to face her.

'Yes, Mrs Jones.'

'What do you think you are doing?'

'Checking my phone. Class is over, right?'

'Class isn't over until you leave this studio,' Mrs Jones said. She pointed to his phone. 'Is that why you were finding it so hard to focus today?'

'What do you mean?' Andre said, playing dumb to try to buy himself some more time to figure out an excuse.

'I mean, were you too busy thinking about what might be going on on MySpace or whatever?'

'MySpace?' Andre looked at her, horrified. Everyone knew that MySpace had gone out decades ago, along with pagers and fax machines.

'Yes.' Mrs Jones took a step closer. 'You know, I've a good mind to confiscate that phone of yours.'

Andre stepped back, clutching his phone to

his chest in horror. 'What? No! You can't!'

'Right, well, I'm definitely going to be speaking to your mother about your behaviour,' Mrs Jones replied. 'Maybe she can talk some sense into you.'

'Great,' Andre muttered.

When he was finally able to get back to his dorm room, Andre opened his laptop and went on to Spotted. He deleted all of the new messages from @snarkerella and blocked them from posting comments on the site. Then he changed his security settings so that he had to accept any new comments before they were published. He didn't like having to do that as it would mean yet more work for him but at least it would stop Spotted from becoming a troll's paradise. He lay back on his bed and gazed up at the ceiling. He was so tired. Maybe he could take a quick nap before dinner. But before he had time to even close his eyes his phone started ringing. He looked at the caller display. It was his mum. Oh good, Mrs Jones must have gone straight to her office to snitch on him the minute class ended. He thought about ignoring the call but what was the point? His mum would only end up coming to his room or approaching him in the canteen instead and he'd had way too much humiliation for one day.

'Hey, Mum.'

'Andre, could you come to see me, please?'

No hello, she must be mad.

'What, right now?'

'Yes.'

'OK.' He ended the call and got to his feet, his cheeks burning. *Now* he knew what Anne Boleyn must have felt like on her way to the chopping block.

When he got to his mum's office he found her and Mrs Jones sitting in the leather armchairs by the coffee table. To his surprise and relief they both smiled at him.

'Andre,' Miss Murphy said. 'Come and join us.'

Andre sat down beside them. They were still

smiling. Maybe this wouldn't be so bad after all.

'We're very concerned about you,' Miss Murphy began. 'Mrs Jones has told me what happened in your tap class today, and after History this morning . . .'

'I didn't realize I wasn't allowed to check my phone until I'd left the studio,' Andre started to explain. 'I thought it was OK because class was over.'

'But you weren't at all focused in class,' Mrs Jones said. 'You were repeatedly out of time and it was like you couldn't wait to get to your phone.'

'What's going on, Andre?' Miss Murphy said, gently placing her hand on his arm. 'We want to help.'

Andre sighed. It was so much easier not telling them when they were being mean.

'Is it to do with your blog?' Miss Murphy asked.

'He has a blog?' Mrs Jones raised her eyebrows.

Andre nodded. 'Yes. And yes, that's what I was checking. I'd been getting some horrible comments, Mum. I needed to delete them.'

'Horrible comments from who?' Miss Murphy immediately looked alarmed.

'I don't know.'

'You don't know?'

'It's the internet, Mum. Anyone can post comments.'

Mrs Jones shook her head sympathetically. 'I don't know how you young people cope with the online world, I really don't.' She looked at Miss Murphy. 'We were so lucky not to have to deal with all that when we were students.'

Miss Murphy nodded. 'Tell me about it.'

Andre fought the urge to leap to the internet's defence. They were actually being sympathetic. He needed to milk that sympathy so they wouldn't start telling him off.

'It can be hell on earth,' he said, with what he hoped was the air of a tragic hero.

'Well, we have some news that we think will help cheer you up – and get you refocused on your dance,' Miss Murphy said.

'Oh yeah?' Andre looked at her cautiously. He really couldn't believe how well this was going.

'WEDA have been asked to take part in a show for a charity,' Mrs Jones said. 'I'll be announcing all the details tomorrow.'

'They want us to come up with a dance that reflects the ethos of the charity,' Miss Murphy said.

Andre nodded absently. He wondered if @snarkerella had realized they'd been blocked yet. Then a horrible thought occurred to him. What if they just created a new online persona? Then they'd be able to get around the block. And although other people might not see what they tried to post, Andre would.

'So, what do you say?' Miss Murphy said with a beaming smile.

'I'm sorry, what?'

'Would you like to be heavily involved in the dance?' Mrs Jones asked.

Andre stared at her blankly. 'What dance?'

'The dance for the show,' Miss Murphy said. Her smile faded. 'Have you been listening to what I've been saying?'

'Yes! Of course. Charity. Show. Do I want to be involved?' Andre echoed.

'*Heavily* involved,' Mrs Jones said, with a knowing smile.

What did she mean, heavily involved? Andre guessed she must want him to dance the lead. Great, that was all he needed.

Miss Murphy frowned. 'But for the dance to be a success you can't afford to be distracted.'

'I'm not distracted,' Andre said, wondering how much longer they were going to keep him there. Like an irritating itch, the urge to check his phone was growing by the second.

'Right, that's it,' Miss Murphy said, springing to her feet. 'Hand it over.'

'Hand what over?'

'Your phone.'

'What?' Andre stared at her, horrified.

'You heard me. I want your phone and your laptop. I'm confiscating them for a week.'

'But you can't do that!'

'Yes I can,' Miss Murphy said defiantly, 'I'm your mom *and* your teacher – that gives me double confiscation rights.'

Andre looked at Mrs Jones in despair. Surely she could see how unfair his mum was being. But Mrs Jones was just nodding and smiling sympathetically.

'I think it's for the best, Andre. Just until you're able to get your head straight again and can focus on the dance for the show.'

'But I – this – it's so unfair.'

Miss Murphy continued holding out her hand. 'Come on. Give it to me.'

'But what if there's an emergency? What if I need to call the police – or the fire brigade?'

'In that unlikely event, there are plenty of other phones at WEDA you could use,' his mum said with an annoying grin. Huh, she wouldn't be

71

grinning if he ended up dying tragically in a fire.

'I'll get you a cheap pay as you go, with no internet access.'

'A phone with no internet access?' Andre gasped. He didn't even know they made phones like that any more.

'Hand it over, please.'

Andre took his phone from his pocket. The notification light was flashing. 'Can I just check my emails? Please?'

Miss Murphy shook her head. 'No. I think you need to go cold turkey starting right now.'

'But if you take away my phone you take away my whole life!'

'Oh, Andre, please!' Miss Murphy laughed.

How could she laugh? Andre watched as his mum took his phone over to her desk and locked it in one of the drawers.

'Now I want you to go and fetch your laptop,' she said.

'But how will I get my assignments done?' he

said defiantly. Surely she'd have to back down over this one.

'You can write them by hand,' Miss Murphy replied. 'I'll have a word with your teachers, explain what's going on.'

Explain that you're an evil dictator, Andre thought bitterly.

'Don't worry,' Mrs Jones said. 'When you find out more about this charity show tomorrow you won't give a second thought to what's happening online.'

Yeah right, Andre thought grimly.

'Go on, go and get your laptop,' Miss Murphy said, smiling at him sweetly. He'd had no idea that someone who looked so friendly could be so cruel. Beneath that warm exterior beat a heart of stone. His mum was no better than Henry VIII.

'I can't believe you've taken my phone,' he muttered as he trudged from the room. Now he knew what Anne Boleyn must have felt like when she lost her head.

CHAPTER SIX

Andre trudged back to the dorm block, his heart heavy and his spirits low. All he wanted to do was crawl into bed and hide away from everyone and everything until his tyrant queen of a mother gave him his phone back. It was all right for old folks like his mum and Mrs Jones – they'd been born before the internet was invented. They could remember what life was like without it. But Andre couldn't imagine a world that was totally offline. The online world *was* his world – without it everything else felt pointless. As he got to his dorm room he heard the sound of laughter and chatter inside. Ugh, just what he needed. He opened the door and saw the rest of Il Bello. MJ and Raf were practising some kind of old-school breakdancing moves on MJ's side of the room and Billie and Tilly were sitting on Andre's bed – Billie was brushing Tilly's hair which had been freshly dyed hot pink.

'Hey, guys,' Andre muttered. He'd never been less enthusiastic about seeing his crew.

'Hey, Dre,' Tilly called. 'What do you think of my hair? I'm channelling my inner flamingo.'

'Yeah, great,' Andre said, going over to his desk and getting his laptop.

'What's up?' Billie said, instantly looking concerned.

'Yeah, what's happened?' Tilly asked. 'Don't you like it? Do you think it's too bright?'

'It's not your hair,' Andre said glumly.

'Did you get busted by your mum?' Raf asked, playing with the tiger's eye pendant around his neck.

'You could say that.'

'Oh no, what happened?' Billie asked.

'Mrs Jones snitched on me,' Andre replied. He looked at his laptop. Maybe he could quickly check on Spotted before he handed his laptop in to his mum.

'What for?' Tilly asked.

'Messing up in tap – and checking my phone before class was over – even though it *was* over. We'd finished dancing.'

'That was a tough break, bro,' Raf said, nodding sympathetically.

'Yeah, well, turns out that was nothing,' Andre said bitterly.

'What do you mean?' MJ stopped roboting and stared at Andre.

'My mum's confiscating all of my online devices.'

Billie and Tilly gasped in unison, Raf's mouth fell open in shock and even the normally super-cool MJ scratched his head. Seeing their stunned reactions made Andre feel just the slightest bit better. He was right to feel so down – what his mum was doing was so mean.

'Why would she do that?' MJ asked.

'She thinks I need to do a digital detox,' Andre

replied. 'She's already got my phone. Now I have to take her my laptop.'

'But that's so harsh,' Billie said.

'Yeah.' Tilly nodded. 'Why does she think you need to do a detox?'

'Because she wants me to focus on my dancing and my school work. She thinks I'm getting too stressed over Spotted.'

'Oh man!' Raf came over and put his arm round Andre's shoulders.

'Yeah, I think it's safe to say that this is the worst day of my entire life.' Andre was starting to quite enjoy all the sympathy he was getting. It was the thinnest silver lining in his cloud of despair. 'Anyway, I'd better go get my laptop over to my mum. She told me I only had five minutes. Thanks, guys. Thanks for everything.' He left the others in a hushed silence – much to his satisfaction.

When Andre got back to his room after dropping off his laptop he thought the others might have gone to dinner but instead he found them all arranging duvets and sleeping bags on the floor.

'What's going on?' he asked.

'We're having an Il Bello sleepover,' Tilly announced. 'We're all staying here tonight.'

'Even me,' Billie said, grinning excitedly. 'I called my mum and explained what had happened and she said it was fine.'

'But why?' Andre looked at them blankly.

'To support you in the first night of your detox, bro,' Raf said.

'Yeah, we reckoned the first night was bound to be the hardest so we thought you could do with some moral support,' Tilly said. 'We're going to order pizza and play some games.'

'What kind of games?' Andre sat down on the only available space at the end of his bed.

'Old-style games,' Billie replied. 'You know, like charades and I-spy. Anything other than going online, basically.'

'Oh, right.' Andre's heart sank. As much as

he appreciated their show of support he'd have preferred if they were trying to help him cheat on his detox. He'd been kind of hoping one of them would lend him their phone. 'I was wondering . . .' he said, looking at Tilly. He figured she'd be the most likely to help him seeing as she was his assistant on Spotted. 'Could you lend me your phone for a bit, just so I can check on the blog?'

Tilly's face fell. 'Oh – uh – I don't know . . .'

'What do you mean, you don't know?'

'Well, it's just that . . .' Her face flushed and she looked away. 'I think your mum might actually have a point.'

'What?' Andre stared at her, horrified. He'd expected this kind of treachery from a teacher . . . but from Tilly? She was supposed to be one of his best friends.

'We all do, bro,' Raf said, coming to sit next to Andre. 'You've been acting kind of stressed lately.'

'Yeah, and you've really been letting the blog get

to you,' Tilly the Treacherous added, still not able to look at him.

'And it has put you off your dance,' Billie added.

'And made you pace up and down this room at night,' MJ said.

Andre looked around at them all. He couldn't believe what he was hearing.

'I got you this,' Raf said, handing Andre a pale pink crystal. 'It's rose quartz. It has great healing properties. All you need to do is hold it whenever you need strength and protection.'

'Thanks,' Andre muttered, stuffing the crystal into his pocket without really looking at it.

'We love you, Dre,' Tilly said, finally making eye contact with him. 'We just want you to be happy.'

'But helping me to get back online would make me happy,' Andre said. 'It would make me very happy.'

'No it wouldn't,' the others all chorused, like they'd been rehearsing this response while he'd been gone.

Andre sighed. It looked as if he was going to have

to go along with this stupid detox – for tonight at least. He supposed they did have his best interests at heart – despite being massively misguided. 'OK then. Who's ordering the pizza?'

Later that night Andre lay in bed desperately trying to stay awake. He was so tired from all the stress of the last few days and his eyelids felt as if they were weighted with stones but he had to stay awake. Once he was sure the others were all asleep he could sneak one of their phones and do a quick email and Spotted check. It had been hours since he'd last been online – anything could have happened. @snarkerella could have set up loads of different profiles and launched a multiple trolling attack. More people could have unsubscribed. Or maybe that joker @fashattack had got in on the action. He hadn't felt that bad before they'd gone to bed. It had actually been quite good fun playing all the old-school games but now the got-to-go-online itch was back and he had to scratch it. He wondered if the others were all asleep. The room was deadly silent, so that was promising. He slowly sat up and looked around in the dark. Raf, Tilly and Billie were in sleeping bags on the floor. It would be too dangerous to get out of bed as he'd probably end up treading on one of them. But if he could just lean out and grab Tilly's bag . . .

He leaned forward and stretched for the bag. It was hard to make out exactly where it was in the dark. He kept leaning and then felt himself lose his balance. 'Aaaarrgh!' he yelped as he toppled head-first on top of Tilly.

'Oof!' she yelled, scrabbling to sit upright. 'What are you doing?'

'What's going on?' Raf muttered sleepily.

'Are you guys OK?' Billie asked.

MJ turned on his bedside lamp. They all stared at Andre, lying splat on top of Tilly.

'Oh my God! What are you guys doing?' Billie said.

'Andre jumped on me,' Tilly replied.

'I didn't jump, I fell,' Andre said, trying desperately to get himself upright.

'Oh yeah?' Raf said with a chuckle.

'Is there something you guys need to tell us?' Billie giggled.

'OMG, no!' Andre said. 'It wasn't Tilly I was trying to get to. It was . . .'

They all looked at him.

'Her phone,' Andre muttered sheepishly.

'I knew it!' Tilly said. 'I knew you'd pull a stunt like this. Right, everyone, put your phones under your bedding so Andre can't get them.'

'There's no need to –'

'Er, hello?' Tilly glared at him. 'I think there's every need.'

'Please, someone. I just need to borrow a phone for five minutes. I'll pay you. Raf?'

But Raf shook his head. 'Sorry, bro. You're gonna have to go cold turkey.'

'You'll thank us for this one day,' MJ said, placing his phone and laptop under his duvet.

'Oh yeah? How'd you figure that one out?'

'I read an interview with a drug addict once – when he was in recovery – and he thanked his family and friends for not giving him the money to score his drugs.'

'Oh my God. I am not a drug addict!'

'Yeah, but you are an internet junkie,' Tilly said, taking her phone from her bag and stuffing it into her sleeping bag.

'Bill?' Andre looked at her pleadingly. But it was no good. Billie was also putting her phone into her sleeping bag.

'Sorry, Dre.' She smiled at him sympathetically. 'It's for your own good.'

MJ turned his lamp out and the room fell silent – apart from the bitter thoughts echoing in Andre's head.

The next morning Andre filed into assembly with the rest of the crew feeling like a zombie. After the drama with the phones it had taken him ages to get off to sleep – he'd been so worked up about what might be happening over on the blog he couldn't get his brain to switch off. He watched as Mrs Jones made her way up on to the stage. As the students all fell quiet she began to speak.

'Good morning, everyone,' she said with a smile. 'Today I'm delighted to be able to share some very exciting news.'

Andre had completely forgotten about the charity show. He wished he could feel excited about it but right now everything was cast in gloom.

'The charity Cool Earth are having a fund-raising show in London,' Mrs Jones continued. 'In Sadler's Wells, no less – and they've asked WEDA to take part.'

A murmur of excitement rippled around the hall, completely bypassing Andre. He'd heard of Cool Earth before but he couldn't remember where – he had way too much else on his mind.

'For those of you who don't know, Cool Earth work tirelessly to save the rainforest to try to stop the destruction of this beautiful planet that we live on,' Mrs Jones continued. 'So it's an absolute honour to be asked to take part in such a worthwhile cause.'

Tilly nudged Andre. 'Isn't it great?' she whispered.

Andre nodded but to him it felt far from great. Dancing in a show like this would be yet another thing to stress over.

'They'd like us to put on a dance that demonstrates the ethos of coming together to help save the planet,' Mrs Jones said. 'And I realized that this isn't just a wonderful opportunity for you as dancers but it's also a wonderful opportunity for you to create a piece from scratch. So with that in mind, I'm delighted to announce that Andre Murphy will be creating and choreographing the show for WEDA – with the full help and support of the teaching staff when needed, of course. It's important to give our students opportunities to grow as choreographers and creators as well as dancers and we'd like to give Andre a chance to focus his attention on what matters most as a dance artist.'

What the hell? Andre's mouth fell open. Led by Mr Marlo and Il Bello, the other students started whooping and clapping.

'Oh, Dre, that's amazing!' Billie gasped as Tilly hugged him.

Cassandra turned from her seat in front of him and treated him to one of her frostiest glares.

Andre felt like telling her not to worry – he wasn't exactly delighted that he'd been given this job either. How was he going to choreograph a dance for a show at Sadler's Wells when he had so much else going on? There wasn't enough room in his head. There wasn't enough time in the day. His excitement and enthusiasm had left the building.

CHAPTER
SEVEN

For the rest of the morning Andre felt as if all of his worst fears had gathered around him like a swarm of wasps, buzzing in his ears. *What if @snarkerella's been trolling Spotted again? What if other people – nice people – have tried to comment but I haven't been able to publish them? What if people get bored of Spotted while I'm on my digital detox and unsubscribe? Everyone knows that to build an online empire you have to be posting online every day. What if I start losing followers on my Instagram and Twitter too? Oh no! What if @snarkerella has discovered my other social media accounts? What if they're trolling me on there right now, in front of everyone, and there's NOTHING I CAN DO!*

By the time the bell rang for lunch Andre could

barely think straight. Maybe he needed to channel his fears into dance like he'd done the other day. He set off for the Stable Studio, hoping that the rest of Il Bello wouldn't need anything from him and they'd let him freestyle for a bit. When he got to the studio he found the crew all huddled together in the centre of the room, chatting excitedly. As soon as they saw him they started to cheer – something that would normally make Andre's day, but today filled him with dread.

'Well done, Dre!' Tilly called.

'We're so proud of you,' Billie said.

'Come over here, bro.' Raf beckoned him. 'We've just been having a brainstorm about the charity show. We've got some sick ideas for you.'

MJ moonwalked over to Andre and shook his hand. 'Really proud of you, Dre,' he said. He looked so serious and sincere it made Andre want to cry.

'We've googled Cool Earth cos, you know, you aren't able to,' Billie said with an awkward smile. 'And we've pulled out some key themes from their website to use as inspiration for your dance.'

'It's so amazing what they're doing.' Tilly looked down at her sketch pad. 'It's even given me an idea for a new mural.'

'It's such a great idea,' Billie said. 'Come and look at what she's done, Dre.'

Andre trudged over and looked at Tilly's sketch book. She'd drawn the image of a hand, which she'd coloured bright red, with the words WE ARE ONE printed beneath it in black.

'It's going to be an interactive piece,' Tilly explained. 'People can place *their* hand on top of the painted hand, to symbolize how we're all connected.'

'Right.' Andre stared at the design blankly. Tilly might as well have been talking in Russian, he didn't have any space in his brain to take in what she was saying. All he could think about was what might be happening online. Then he had a brainwave. He could go to the LRC – log on to one of the computers there. Why hadn't he thought of that before?

'I – uh – I have to go,' he stammered.

MJ frowned. 'But you just got here.'

'Yeah,' Tilly said, putting her pad down and looking hurt.

'We've got so much to talk about,' Billie said.

Andre stared around the studio as if he was searching for an excuse. 'I just remembered – I have a History detention.'

'You do?' Raf frowned at him.

'Yeah, after what happened in class the other day. You know, when I told Mr Benson that I thought History was irrelevant. He gave me a detention. I must have forgotten to tell you.'

Raf shook his head sympathetically. 'Bad luck, man.'

'Thanks.' Andre started making his way over to the door.

'Shall we meet after school instead?' Billie asked, running after him.

'Er, yeah, OK. I'll see you later.' Andre hurried out of the Stable Studio and back up to the old building. He pictured the row of computers in the LRC waiting for him. They were like a light at the end of a very dark tunnel.

As soon as he got to the library he went over to one of the computers and quickly entered his student number to gain internet access. A message popped up in the middle of the screen. ACCESS DENIED it said, in angry red letters. Andre sighed. In his rush to get online he must have entered the incorrect number. He tried again, this time making sure every digit he entered was correct. But once again a message flashed up saying ACCESS DENIED. Andre's stomach churned. Surely his mum wouldn't have had him blocked? Surely she wouldn't be that cruel? He tried once more. And once more, he was denied access.

'What the hell?' he said loudly.

'Shhh!' A passing librarian glared at him.

Andre stared at the message on the screen. This was outrageous. This kind of censorship only happened in dictatorships, not at the World

Elite Dance Academy. His human rights were being violated! Maybe he should contact Amnesty International . . .

'Andre! What are you doing?'

Andre spun round and saw Billie standing right behind him, hands on hips.

'I thought you had a History detention.'

'I did – I just had to – er . . .' Andre shifted to try to block Billie's view of the screen.

'Were you online?' Billie said, looking round him.

'No,' Andre muttered, gazing sheepishly into his lap.

'Then what are you doing on a computer?' Billie grabbed a nearby chair and sat down next to him.

'I haven't been online, I swear. I wasn't able to. My mother has blocked me.'

'She's what?' Billie's bright green eyes widened in shock.

'Look.' Andre pointed at the message on the screen.

'Wow. She must be super-serious about this detox.'

'She is. She's an evil dictator and she –'

'Shhhh!' the librarian said, as she walked back past them.

'Great,' Andre said. 'Everyone's trying to silence me. Welcome to the WEDA dictatorship.'

'OK, let's get out of here,' Billie said, getting to her feet.

'And go where?' Andre said dejectedly. 'I'm sorry, Bill, but I can't face going back to the Stable Studio. I can't see the others right now.'

'We're not going back to the studio. We're going for a walk,' Billie said. 'My Uncle Charlie always says that walking is like meditating with your feet.'

'What's that supposed to mean?' Andre asked.

'I'm not exactly sure. He got the idea from one of his trips to Peru. But Uncle Charlie is one of the happiest people I know and he walks loads so it must do some good.'

'OK,' Andre said with a sigh. At least going outside might give him a chance to clear his head. He followed Billie out of the old building and they started walking along the winding drive, away from the academy.

'So come on, Dre,' Billie said, linking her arm in his. 'Tell me what's going on. Why are you so stressed? And I'm not talking about the digital detox – you were stressing out before then. What's wrong?'

Andre stared straight ahead of him as they walked. He wasn't sure if it was the fact that he didn't have to make eye contact with Billie that made it easier but suddenly he felt the overwhelming urge to open up and tell her exactly how he was feeling.

'I – I feel like my head's going to explode,' he said quietly. He felt her grip his arm tighter.

'Why?'

'Because – because I've got so much going on in there. So much to worry about . . .'

'Like what?' Billie asked gently.

'Like the blog, and getting trolled, and people unsubscribing, and not getting enough followers. And then there's this place.' He gestured to the WEDA grounds. 'They expect so much from us.

And some of the classes, like History, well, they feel like such a waste of time.'

'How do you mean?'

'Why do we need to study what went on in the past?' Now Andre had started to open up to Billie he couldn't stop. All of his frustration came pouring out. 'It just feels so irrelevant when I'm trying so hard to build my future. I don't have the head-space to think about some king who lived, like, hundreds of years ago. And now they want me to choreograph this charity dance on top of everything else and I just don't have the time.'

'But, Dre, you can't pull out of the show – it's for Cool Earth.'

'Yes, I know it's a great cause but I –'

'It's for *Cool Earth*,' Billie interrupted, her eyes sparkling with excitement. 'You know, the charity that has your fashion hero as a patron.'

Andre looked at her blankly.

'Vivienne Westwood,' Billie said. 'She's one of their main supporters.'

'Oh my God!' Andre clamped his hand to his mouth. That was why Cool Earth had sounded familiar. Vivienne Westwood sometimes mentioned them in interviews but Andre had been so stressed out he'd completely forgotten. He could feel his heart beating rapidly with excitement. This was a *major* opportunity for him and WEDA. Suddenly he had tingles like never before!

'And you have got enough time to choreograph the dance,' Billie added.

'How?'

'Well, now you're on a digital detox you're going to save loads of time.' Billie stopped walking. 'How often do you normally go online in a day?'

'I don't know.' Andre frowned as he tried to do the maths, but it was impossible. He went online all the time, constantly flicking between his social media accounts and blog. That was why he was finding it so damn hard to be without the internet. 'A lot,' he said.

'Like, every couple of hours?'

Andre shook his head. 'No, more than that.'

'Right. So, if you added up all that time over the course of a day do you reckon it would come to hours?'

Andre nodded.

Billie grinned. 'So, while you're on this digital detox you're going to have hours of extra time every day.'

'Well, yeah, I guess.'

'Extra time that you could spend on choreographing the dance for the show?'

Andre nodded.

'And catching up on your History homework.'

Andre grimaced.

'History isn't irrelevant, Dre, seriously. Everything that happens in the present and the future is down to whatever happened in the past. And fashion and dance are great examples of that.' Billie gazed off into the distance thoughtfully. Then her face broke into a smile. 'I've got a great idea.'

Andre shoved his hands in his pockets to keep

them warm. 'Oh yeah? Does it involve hacking the WEDA computer system and getting me internet access?'

'No! I'm going to take you somewhere. Somewhere really cool. It'll help you see how important History is *and* give you something to do on your digital detox.' She re-linked arms with him. 'Trust me, Dre, you're going to love it.'

As they carried on walking Andre felt the slightest glimmer of hope. He very much doubted that anywhere Billie could take him would make him like History – it would be like trying to convert Dr Dre to country and western music. But what the hell, at least it would give him a distraction from his troubles.

CHAPTER EIGHT

The next day, Andre met Billie outside South Kensington tube station.

'I made you something,' she said, pressing an envelope into his hand. 'It's also a clue to where I'm taking you.'

Andre opened the envelope and pulled out a home-made card. Billie had drawn the outline of a fashion mannequin on the front and written a quote above it in green and gold.

'*In history people dressed much better than we do today,*' he read aloud.

Billie smiled. 'It's from your hero, Vivienne Westwood.'

'Really?'

Billie nodded. Then she stood in front of him and folded her arms, a determined expression upon her face. 'My mission today is to make you see that what happened in the past is extremely relevant to what's happening in the present. Follow me.'

Andre followed as she began marching through the throng of tourists. South Kensington was a hub for museums so it was always crowded. 'Where are we going?' he asked.

Billie pointed to an ornate, grey stone building across the road.

'The V&A!' Andre grinned as he read the sign outside. He'd only been to the Victoria and Albert museum once before, several years ago with his mum. He couldn't remember much about it now but he knew that he'd loved it.

'They've got a really cool exhibition on at the moment,' Billie explained. 'It's on Tudor fashion. I thought that if you saw how people dressed back then it might make your Tudor History lessons more interesting.'

'OK,' Andre said, as he dodged between a taxi and a doubler-decker bus and followed her across the road. He wasn't sure Billie's plan would work but it could be interesting anyway. They made their way up the sweeping stone steps at the front of the museum and into the lobby.

'Oh man, it's like being inside a palace!' Andre exclaimed, taking in the huge domed ceiling and white stone archways. A fabulous chandelier made from intricate spirals of blue and yellow glass hung above the reception desk.

'Come on,' Billie said. 'We need to go up to the first floor.'

Andre followed her through a pair of shiny marble pillars and up a flight of stairs. They walked along a gallery full of exotic statues of mythical creatures and gods.

'This place is dope!' Andre gasped.

'Wait till you see the clothes,' Billie replied with a grin.

They went through a set of doors at the end

of the gallery and into a large, darkened room. Spotlights fell upon rows of mannequins, all clad in Tudor dress.

'Hmm,' Andre said, as he looked at the first exhibit. It was a mannequin of a young man. He was wearing a plain woollen tunic over a pair of short trousers and woollen socks that came up to the knee. 'Tudor fashion was pretty basic.'

'For the poor people,' Billie said. 'But wait till you see what the rich people wore.'

They walked over to the next exhibit – the mannequin of a Tudor peasant woman. She was wearing a plain brown dress made from wool and a white linen apron. Andre made a mental note to not ever feature Tudor Peasant Chic on Spotted and instantly felt a twinge of anxiety. It had been almost an entire day since he'd last checked his blog. He'd never gone this long without checking before. All hell could be breaking loose. He took a deep breath and pushed the anxious thoughts from his mind. There was nothing he could do about it so he might as well just enjoy being at the museum.

'Wow, look at this,' Billie said, making her way over to the next exhibit. It was of a weird, white hooped skirt. The hoops got wider as they reached the floor. 'Women had to wear one of these underneath their dresses,' Billie said, reading from a sign next to the exhibit. 'How did they sit down in them?'

'I have no idea,' Andre replied. 'Oh gross, the hoops were made of whale-bone!'

Billie bounded off to the next exhibit, a glass case displaying different headwear. 'Look at this cap,' she said. 'It's just like something Tillz would make.'

Andre examined the cap. It was made from dark blue velvet and decorated with feathers and jewels. 'OMG, that is so Tillz!' he exclaimed. 'I've got to get a picture of it for her.' He automatically reached into his pocket for his phone. 'Oh yeah.'

'Don't worry, I'll take one for her.' Billie got her phone out and took a picture. Andre looked at it wistfully, like someone on a diet drooling over a cream cake. Billie hastily stuffed her phone back in her bag. 'OK, what's next?'

They walked over to the next exhibit. Andre recognized the huge, bearded mannequin instantly. It was Henry VIII. He was wearing a fur-trimmed, scarlet coat over a gold tunic and white tights. There was a heavy gold chain draped across his shoulders.

'Can you believe that Henry VIII used to dress like that?' Billie said.

'I know he was, like, a psycho wife-killer,' Andre said, gazing up at the mannequin, 'but he definitely had swag, didn't he?'

'I suppose,' Billie said. 'But I prefer his daughter. I think she was the original Vivienne Westwood.'

Andre frowned at her. 'What do you mean, the original Vivienne Westwood?'

'Look . . .' Billie led Andre over to a mannequin of Elizabeth I.

'Wowser!' Andre gasped. The mannequin looked amazing. Elizabeth's flame-coloured hair was so striking against her milky-white face. A huge ruff decorated with pearls fanned out around her head. Her dress was like a work of art – pale gold silk, adorned with scarlet bows, embroidered flowers and pearls shaped like teardrops. Six long strings of pearls hung from her neck right down to her waist. Billie was right. With her pale skin and orange hair, she did look like Vivienne Westwood – or rather Vivienne Westwood looked like Elizabeth. Andre felt a wave of relief. Maybe it was impossible for *anyone* to be truly original. Even Vivienne Westwood. @snarkerella was wrong to have called Andre a wannabe. Andre had never copied anyone outright. He'd used other people as inspiration and added his own unique twist, just as Vivienne Westwood had done. He looked at the mannequin of Elizabeth and smiled. Then, the weirdest thing happened. Ideas started popping into his head, like rough sketches appearing in a pad. He could do an Elizabethan-inspired feature for Spotted. He could have a girl in a ruff and dress and pearls but teamed with a pair of Docs to give it a modern twist. He could have a guy – Raf, maybe – in Tudor-style tracksuit bottoms, customized with scarlet and gold brocade. He could get Tillz to make him a Tudor-style cap, accessorized with feathers and costume jewellery. Andre grinned. He hadn't felt this fired up in ages. He needed to make a note of his ideas so he didn't forget them.

'Bill, do you have some paper and a pen?' he asked.

'No, why?'

'I'm getting some ideas for new looks,' he explained.

'Really?' Billie's face lit up. 'I bet they have notepads and pens in the gift shop. Shall we go and see? Then we could get a coffee in the cafe and you could write them all down.'

'Awesome plan.' Andre gave Elizabeth I an appreciative wink, then headed after Billie.

Once Andre had bought a V&A notepad and pen – and postcards of Henry VIII and Elizabeth I – he and Billie headed for the cafe.

'OMG!' he exclaimed as they walked in. 'Major interior design goals.'

The restaurant was huge, lined with dark red wallpaper and a gold trim running along the ceiling and archways. Four huge white and gold pillars formed a square in the centre of the room, with neatly laid tables dotted all around.

'Apparently this was the first ever museum restaurant in the world,' Billie told him, as they made their way through to the cafe.

'You're kidding.' Andre gazed around the room. It felt so cool to be standing in such a historic place.

'See, history isn't so bad after all,' Billie said, giving him a playful nudge.

'No. I guess it isn't.'

They ordered coffees and sat on a terrace overlooking a beautiful courtyard garden. Andre jotted down his Tudor-inspired fashion ideas then he sat back and drank in the view. He guessed nothing much had changed since the museum was first built. He pictured people in olden-day clothes strolling around the garden, the women twirling their parasols, the men adjusting their hats. And for the first time ever he didn't see the olden days as something completely separate from him. Everything that had happened in the past had gone on to inspire the next thing. You could see it through fashion . . . and you could see it through dance. Another idea popped into his head – what if he choreographed a piece for the Cool Earth show that showed dance throughout the ages all the way up to the present day . . .? He started scribbling in his pad again. He could use dance to show how things had changed and how the planet was now suffering because of the destruction of the rainforest.

'What are you writing now?' Billie asked. 'More fashion ideas?'

Andre shook his head. 'No, dance ideas – for the show.' He stopped writing and smiled at her. 'Thanks so much for bringing me here, Bill. You've helped me see things clearly again.'

Billie leaped to her feet, leaned across the table and hugged him tightly. 'I am so, so happy to hear that, Dre!'

When Andre and Billie got back to WEDA they headed straight for the Stable Studio. Andre had got Billie to text the others when they were on the train to tell them that he needed to see them urgently. This time, he'd only felt the slightest wistful pang when he saw her on her phone – his head was filling with so many new ideas he didn't have room to be sad any more.

When they got to the studio the others were all standing by the far wall. Tilly was standing in the middle of them, wearing the old paint-splattered tracksuit she always wore when she was doing her graffiti art.

'Yay, you're back!' Tilly exclaimed as soon as she saw them. 'Come and see what I've done.'

She'd painted the wall red, with a large black hand design in the centre. Beneath the hand she'd sprayed the words WE ARE ONE in her signature graffiti style.

'Wow!' gasped Billie.

'What do you think?' Tilly asked, looking at Andre nervously.

'Tillz, it's awesome.' A scene flashed into Andre's head – a stage filled with dancers all wearing T-shirts with the same design on them. 'Would you be able to get this design printed on some T-shirts?'

'Of course,' Tilly replied. 'What for?'

'For the Cool Earth show.'

'The Cool Earth show?' Tilly echoed. 'You mean, you want to do it now?'

'Of course I want to do it,' Andre replied.

Raf and MJ whooped.

'But yesterday . . . you seemed so down,' Tilly said.

'Yeah well, that was yesterday. I was in the grips of cold turkey. I wasn't thinking straight. But thanks to Billie I'm born again. Like a phoenix from the flames, I have risen from the ashes of my internet ban. Older, wiser and badder than ever.'

'Not to mention more OTT than ever,' MJ said drily.

Andre raised one perfectly plucked eyebrow. Then he clapped his hands together. 'Come on, guys, let's get cracking. We've got a show to produce!'

CHAPTER NINE

A couple of days later something really weird happened, something that had never, ever happened to Andre before. He woke up before 7 a.m. – *on a Saturday!* And it wasn't because he was stressed and couldn't sleep – the opposite, in fact. As he lay there, gazing up at the ceiling, he felt more relaxed than he'd done in ages. He'd been four days without the internet now and his head felt clearer than ever. He was acing his dance classes again – even tap – he was on top of his homework – even History – and his plans for the Cool Earth show were coming together brilliantly. In fact, being without his devices had actually helped because he'd had to use other people's playlists to pick the music from.

He'd found some real gems in MJ's collection in particular. Today he had to hold auditions for the lead roles and present his ideas to his mum and Mrs Jones. There was just one thing he still wasn't sure of – the role *he* was going to play in the dance. He decided to go in search of some inspiration.

He got out of bed and pulled on some clothes – drastically cutting his normal posing in front of the mirror time to just five minutes. On the other side of the dorm, MJ was still fast asleep. Andre crept from the room and quietly shut the door behind him. Then he made his way to the reception in the old building. This early on a weekend the corridors at WEDA were deathly quiet. Andre liked having the place to himself for once. It made it easier to think. He wanted to create a role for himself in the charity show that would allow him to express his true self, but what could it be?

When he got to reception he went over to the glass-fronted cabinets lining the wall and studied the spines of the old, leather-bounds books inside.

Finally, he found what he was looking for – a large book titled *The Complete History of Ballet*. He carefully took the book from the shelf and sat down on one of the plush leather sofas. As he flicked through the yellow-tinged pages an illustration caught his eye. It was of a man dressed in a stunning gold costume, with a huge golden headdress radiating from his head. '*King Louis XIV as Apollo*' the caption below read. Andre vaguely remembered being taught about King Louis and how he had helped promote classical ballet in France. As he read the text beneath the picture his heart beat faster. As a teenager, King Louis had performed in *Le Ballet de la Nuit* as Apollo, the god of the sun. After that he was known as the Sun King.

Andre stared at the illustration. King Louis had only been a couple of years older than Andre was now when he'd danced as Apollo. He'd been a pioneer of ballet – daring to follow his passion for dance in spite of being king. He was the ultimate role model for being the three Bs – fearless, authentic and you. Andre pictured himself dancing a tribute to King Louis, dressed as the sun god Apollo, and his skin began to tingle.

The door opened and Mr Marlo came into the reception, a sports bag swung over his muscular shoulder.

'Hey, Andre, whatcha doin?' he said, coming over to the sofa.

'Hey, Mr M. I'm just doing some research for the Cool Earth show.'

'Oh yeah?' Mr Marlo sat down next to him and looked at the book. 'Aha, King Louis. Now there was a dude who was passionate about dance. Did you know he had a ballet lesson every single day?'

Andre shook his head.

'He was definitely a trail-blazer. Because of him all the French dudes wanted to dance.'

Andre looked at the picture of King Louis wistfully. Oh, to be a trail-blazer too. 'I was thinking of maybe dancing a tribute to him in the show, as the Sun King.'

Mr Marlo nodded. 'That sounds like a great idea. Hey, do you want to freestyle a few ideas with me before the rest of this place wakes up?'

'Are you sure?'

'Sure I'm sure.' Mr Marlo got to his feet. 'Come on, let's go to the Murphy Studio. The light in there's great this early.'

Once they got to the studio Andre explained to Mr Marlo that he wanted to choreograph something that showed the history of the planet through the history of dance. 'I want to show how we can change things for the better in the future too,' he added. 'Like, if we all come together to save the rainforest, the orang-utans and other endangered species.'

Mr Marlo smiled enthusiastically. 'I know a great song for that theme.' He took his phone from his pocket. 'Have you heard of Sam Cooke?'

Andre shook his head.

Mr Marlo looked horrified. 'Son, you are about to get a master class in soulful singing. Listen to this. It's called "A Change is Gonna Come".'

Mr Marlo started playing the song. The vocal was so raw and tender it took Andre's breath away. And the lyrics were so poignant they made him well up. He closed his eyes and swayed his head in time to the soaring melody.

'Go on,' Mr Marlo said gently. 'Dance how it makes you feel.'

Andre got to his feet. The song made him ache with a weird mixture of sadness and hope. The sadness he felt for all of the pain on the planet . . . and the hope that Sam Cooke was right, that a change for the better was going to come. He poured his emotions into some contemporary ballet moves, matching the fluidity of the song.

'Bravo!' Mr Marlo said, when the song ended. 'Now, how about we take it from the top and this time you add a bit of the anger you feel about the way the world works. Use the striking rhythms and hits of street dance in contrast to your beautiful lines and expressions through contemporary.' Mr Marlo smiled at Andre. 'This piece is about taking your power back in what seems like a hopeless situation, about owning it and using it to shine your light as bright as you can. Be the beacon of hope people need to believe in a better future.'

The next hour passed by in a blur and by the end of it Andre had a routine he was proud of.

'Thank you so much, Mr M,' he said.

'No problem at all. You're going to knock 'em all dead. Now I'd better go grab some breakfast before my African dance students show up.'

After breakfast Andre and the rest of Il Bello met in the Stable Studio to prepare for the auditions. First up was the audition for the lead ballet role.

'It feels so weird being the auditioner for once.' Billie grinned as she took her seat next to the others behind a makeshift audition desk.

'Yeah, weird and great,' Tilly said, running her fingers over her face. 'No nerves equals no break-out. My skin is eternally grateful to you, Dre.'

Andre laughed. 'Glad to hear it.'

There was a loud knock on the door.

'Come in,' MJ called.

Led by Cassandra, five of the best ballet dancers at WEDA entered the studio. Cassandra looked around. As she took in Tilly's graffiti art she wrinkled her nose as if she could smell something bad.

'This should be fun,' Billie muttered.

'Is it me or did the temperature in here drop the second she walked in?' Tilly whispered.

'OK, guys, we're gonna need to keep it professional,' Andre said. 'I know she's the Ice Queen but she's also WEDA's best ballerina. We're going to have to suck it up for the sake of the show.' He got up and walked over to them. 'Welcome, guys! We're so glad you could all try out for the role.'

Cassandra gave one of her haughty laughs. 'Yeah right, as if you're going to cast anyone other than me.'

Andre took a deep breath. This was going to require a *lot* of sucking it up.

'Wow, who did that?' Cassandra said, looking at Tilly's latest mural. 'It's a little stark, isn't it?'

'It's supposed to be,' Tilly said, marching over.

Andre's heart sank. The last thing he needed was a punch-up before Cassandra had even danced a step.

'Riiiiight,' Cassandra said slowly, like she was humouring a five year old.

'It's interactive,' Billie called out from behind the desk. 'The idea is that people take it in turns to place their hand on top of the image of the hand, to show that we're all connected. Why don't you have a go?'

Cassandra shuddered. 'I don't think so. It could be infectious.'

Andre stared at her blankly. 'What do you mean?'

'Well, you never know where other people's hands have been, do you?' She pulled a face. 'I'm not putting my hand there – I might catch something.'

'Good point, definitely don't touch it,' Tilly said.

Andre looked at her, shocked. Surely Tilly wasn't agreeing with her arch enemy?

'Your personality might be infectious,' Tilly snapped at Cassandra. 'And we wouldn't want anyone catching your attitude problem, would we?' She turned and marched back over to the others.

Andre heard Billie coughing hard to try to disguise a giggle. He took another deep breath and prepared for what was shaping up to be the hardest audition of his life – and he wasn't even the one in the spotlight!

Of course, as soon as the music started playing and Cassandra started dancing, all of Il Bello, even Tilly, watched, mesmerized. They'd chosen the song 'Don't Let the Sun Go Down on Me' for an ensemble piece featuring a ballet solo and Andre had asked the dancers to dance en pointe.

Although Tilly's room-mate Naomi pulled off a pretty impressive performance, Cassandra was clearly in a league of her own, doing triple turns with ease where the others could only do doubles.

She also jumped way higher, landing as lightly as a feather.

'That girl is so confusing,' MJ muttered as they watched Cassandra execute a triple pirouette en pointe, going into the most beautiful arabesque. It was as if she floated and glided across the floor, effortlessly completing moves others only dreamed of. 'I know she's mean in real life but when she dances . . .'

'Tell me about it,' Raf said with a sigh. 'So confusing!'

'OK, boys, no need to drool,' Tilly muttered.

As Andre watched Cassandra dance he could totally relate to MJ and Raf's mixed emotions. Cassandra might be an evil ice queen but right now she was killing it on the dance floor and he knew she'd be one of the stars of the show.

'OK, you've got the part,' he called to Cassandra, as soon as the song ended.

'Ha! I told you this whole audition thing was a farce,' Cassandra said with a triumphant smile, as the others trudged off the dance floor.

'We'll see you at the first rehearsal tomorrow at eleven,' Andre said quickly, wanting to get shot of her before Tilly exploded.

The rest of the auditions went really well and by the end of the day every part was cast. Andre arrived at Mrs Jones's office feeling elated. And thankfully, when he ran through his ideas for the show with Mrs Jones and his mum, they both shared his enthusiasm.

'This all sounds wonderful, Andre,' Mrs Jones exclaimed. 'You've put so much thought into it.'

'And we've been hearing great things from your teachers too,' Miss Murphy said. 'It seems like this digital detox was exactly what you needed.'

'Hmm.' Andre faked a frown but inside he couldn't help agreeing. Things had got a whole lot better these past few days.

'I'm very proud of how hard you've been working,' Miss Murphy said. 'So proud, in fact, that I have a little surprise waiting for you back at the apartment.'

'What kind of surprise?' Andre's skin prickled with excitement.

'Well, if I told you that then it wouldn't be a surprise, would it?' Miss Murphy laughed. 'Come on, let's go and see.'

As Andre followed his mum to her apartment he had a pretty good idea what the surprise was. She was going to give him back his phone and laptop and call a halt to the digital detox. He was surprised at how unexcited he felt at the prospect. It had been so nice to not have to worry about Spotted and trolls and internet stuff for a few days. His mum opened the door to her apartment and ushered him in.

'So – uh – your surprise is in the living room,' she said, taking off her jacket. She seemed slightly nervous. Maybe she was having second thoughts about giving them back.

'OK.' Andre strolled into the living room and

looked around for his phone. 'Oh. My. God.' He stood motionless, his jaw dropping open in shock.

A man was sitting on the settee – a well-built man wearing a plaid shirt, faded jeans and cowboy boots.

Andre gulped. 'Dad. What are you doing here?'

CHAPTER
TEN

'I've come to visit ya, son,' Andre's dad, Joe, said, getting to his feet. He looked even bigger standing up, like a cowboy version of Action Man. He held out a meaty, calloused hand for Andre to shake.

'But why?' Andre stared at him blankly.

'So, er, what do you think of your surprise?' Miss Murphy said anxiously as she came into the room.

'It's – uh – very surprising,' Andre mumbled.

'Your mom said she thought you could do with a little father-son time.' Joe's slow Texan drawl seemed even stronger outside of America. It didn't belong here. *He* didn't belong here. WEDA was where Andre lived with his mum. He'd never seen his dad outside of the US before – he'd managed to keep the two worlds entirely separate and now they'd collided he felt totally thrown off guard. 'She thought it'd be good for us to hang out fer a while,' Joe continued, stuffing his hands into his jeans pockets and looking about as awkward as Andre felt.

'She did?' Andre stared at Miss Murphy, trying to figure out why she would ever have thought such a thing. She knew how strained things got between him and his dad. First she took his phone away and now this. What had got into her?

'I'll just go and finish making dinner,' Miss Murphy said in a sing-song voice, like the three of them were always playing happy families, 'and let you guys catch up.'

Don't leave me here! Andre silently pleaded, as if he was sending her a psychic text message. But it seemed that even his psychic messages had been blocked. Totally oblivious to her son's desperate plight, Miss Murphy hurried off out of the room. Andre looked around helplessly. He had no idea how to deal with this mother (or rather, *father*) of all curve balls.

The last time he'd seen his dad had been during the Christmas holidays. He and his mum had flown to Dallas to have an early Christmas dinner with his dad's folks, before going to New York for the rest of the holidays. It had been a total awkward-fest. Joe was from a wealthy Texan family who'd made their fortune in the oil industry. Joe's dad, Andre's granddad, Sam, had invested some of that fortune in the American Ballet, which was how his parents had first met. Fifteen years ago, Joe had accompanied Sam to a performance of *Swan Lake*, in which Miss Murphy had been principal dancer. Joe and Miss Murphy had met backstage and apparently it had been love at first sight. Unfortunately, that love had faded as soon as Andre was born. Joe had wanted Miss Murphy to give up her career as a dancer to be a stay-at-home mum. Refusing to give up on her passion for dance, Miss Murphy had taken the job at WEDA and she and Andre had relocated to the UK, five thousand miles away from Joe Hackett and all of his macho-man rubbish. Until now. Andre glanced at Joe. Joe was studying the tips of his cowboy boots like they contained the cure for cancer. Geez, could this situation be any more awkward?

'So – uh – how long are you in the UK for?' Andre asked, praying that the answer would fall somewhere below twenty-four hours.

'A couple a weeks,' Joe replied.

'A couple of weeks?' Andre stared at him in horror. A couple of weeks was fourteen days. And although Maths wasn't his strongest subject, he knew that fourteen days equalled hundreds of hours, and thousands of minutes! And the worst thing was, whenever he was with his dad it was like time slowed down to a snail's crawl. So really, fourteen days in father-son time would be like four hundred days in normal time. Holy cow, this was a total nightmare! Then another horrendous thought invaded Andre's mind. 'Where are you staying?' he asked, praying the answer wasn't WEDA.

'A hotel in London,' Joe replied.

Andre bit on his lip to stop himself from crying out with relief. This was something at least.

'So, how have ya been?' Finally, Joe peeled his gaze from his boots to look at his son. Andre could feel the burn of his stare as it took in his gold tracksuit bottoms, leopard print tank and fluorescent pink high-tops. Joe was the only person in the world who was able to make Andre doubt his own style. It drove him nuts. Especially as Joe's idea of fabulous was a Stetson hat and double-denim. He took a deep breath and quickly reminded himself of the three Bs. *Be fearless. Be authentic. Be you.*

'Good. I've been so good,' Andre replied, instantly wanting to kick himself. This was another thing he hated about Joe, the way he got on edge when he was with him and ended up saying the lamest things, like, 'I've been so good.'

'Awesome.'

Another silence fell. Andre felt as if the awkwardness was choking him.

'It's just that your mom said . . .' Joe broke off and went back to studying his boots.

'She said what?' Andre prickled. He knew that other parents, *married* parents, would discuss their kids together but he was used to his mum and dad being totally separate. He didn't like the thought of them talking about him one bit.

'She said you'd been having a tough time of it.'

'A tough time of what?'

'School . . . and she said somethin' about a blog?' Joe said this last bit as if he were asking a question, like he didn't really understand.

'Did she show you my blog?' Andre shuddered at the thought of Joe reading Spotted; of him scratching his buzz cut in bewilderment at the harem-pants post. Why had his mum done this to him? It was like she was on a mission to make his life hell.

'No,' Joe replied. 'She just told me you'd been under a lot of pressure. So, what's the blog about?'

Andre imagined the kind of blogs Joe would like reading. Websites with names like *Oil News Daily* or

Cowboy.com. He thought about making something up – inventing a blog his dad might approve of, but he couldn't do it. He'd be breaking the three Bs' code. 'It's about fashion,' he muttered, staring at the door and willing his mum to come through it and save him from this nightmare.

'Fashion?' Joe said the word like he was spitting out some sour lemon.

'Yeah.' Andre continued looking at the door but he could feel Joe's stare burning into him.

'What kind of fashion?'

Geez, could this be any more painful? 'Uh – clothes fashion.'

'I see.'

Andre could just imagine what Joe must be thinking. He had enough of a problem with the fact that his son was a dancer. Now knowing that his son was also a fashion blogger would probably tip him over the edge.

'Dinner's ready!' Miss Murphy called from the other room.

Andre and Joe leaped to their feet, both clearly as desperate as each other to get out of The. Conversation. From. Awkward. Hell.

Andre followed Joe into the dining room. Three places had been laid at the table, with three plates of chilli steaming away. Miss Murphy was standing behind her chair, looking at them anxiously.

'Take a seat,' she said.

They all sat down.

'Great – chilli con carne,' Joe said, looking down at his plate, removing his Stetson hat in true cowboy fashion.

'*Vegan* chilli,' Miss Murphy corrected.

'Say what?' Joe's mouth dropped open in shock.

'Vegan chilli.' Miss Murphy smiled at him.

'But how can chilli be vegan?' Joe gawped at her like she'd just announced there was life on Mars.

'I used tofu mince instead of beef.'

Andre sat back and watched this latest development with interest. His meat-loving dad had steak for breakfast, lunch and dinner. How would he take this news?

'What the heck is tofu?' Joe asked.

'It's a vegetable protein,' Andre explained.

'But why would you have a vegetable protein when you could have meat?'

Andre shrugged. 'Oh I don't know – to stave off heart disease? To lose weight? To save the planet from imminent destruction?'

'It's really great,' Miss Murphy said quickly. 'Try it. You'd hardly know that it isn't meat.'

Joe looked at her, then down at his plate. Very slowly and clearly reluctantly, he took a forkful of chilli. Andre watched, no longer caring if things got super-awkward. He wanted his mum to see exactly how much of a dumb idea this had been. Joe swallowed hard and took a swig from his bottle of beer.

'That's disgustin'!' he spluttered. 'It's got no taste at all.'

'How can something be disgusting if it's got

no taste at all?' Andre asked. 'I mean, sure, if it tastes like rotten eggs or mouldy ditch water, then you can call it disgusting, but if it's got *no* taste how –'

'It's just that you aren't used to it,' Miss Murphy interrupted, smiling sweetly at Joe.

Andre glared. Why was she being so nice to him when he'd just been so mean about her cooking?

'When Andre first became vegan I had my reservations,' his mum continued, 'but I feel so much better for it.'

'You're a vegan?' Joe stared at Andre as if he was an alien. The disappointment in his eyes was too much for Andre to bear. All of his pent-up frustration came bubbling up to the surface.

'Yes, Dad. I'm vegan, I'm a dancer, I blog about fashion . . . and I'm gay! And you might not like that but guess what? This is my home you're in now. So if you can't be polite then don't say anything at all.' Andre got to his feet. 'I'm sorry, Mum. I've lost my appetite.'

'Andre, don't go!' Miss Murphy also stood up, looking distraught. But Andre couldn't stay there a second longer. She'd invited Joe to come and visit, she could deal with him. He marched out into the hall.

'Andre!' Miss Murphy came running after him and grabbed his arm. 'Please!'

'Please what, Mum?' Andre turned to her, tears burning in his eyes. 'Please stay and see what a huge disappointment I am to my own dad? Why would I want to do that? Why did you ask him to come here?'

'I thought it might do you good.' Miss Murphy sighed.

'How? How could that possibly do me any good?'

'If you saw how much he cares about you.'

'How much he cares about me?' Andre looked at her incredulously. 'He doesn't care about me. You saw him in there. He couldn't be more disappointed in me if he tried.'

Miss Murphy shook her head. 'That's not

true, Andre. It's just that you and he are very different people.'

'Er, yeah.'

Joe stepped out into the hall and cleared his throat. 'I'm sorry, son. I didn't mean for things to get off on the wrong foot like that. I really do want us to spend some more time together.'

'What's the point?' Andre said glumly. 'We'll only end up fighting again, like we always do.'

'But I don't want us to always end up fighting. I want us to get to know each other better.' Joe smiled at him. It was slightly tense around the edges but it was a smile nonetheless. 'Tell ya what, how 'bout we go out tomorrow night in London? My treat, but you choose where we go – show me what you like to do.'

Andre stared at him, waiting for him to reveal some kind of catch. 'Seriously?'

'Uh-huh.'

'And you won't make any digs about me being vegan or a dancer or anything . . .'

'I promise.'

'OK then – I guess.'

'That's a wonderful idea.' Miss Murphy grinned with relief. 'Now come on in and finish dinner.'

Andre shook his head. 'No thanks. I'm really not hungry and I've got a load of homework to do.'

Miss Murphy sighed. 'All right then, darling. So I'll see you tomorrow?'

'Yep. See you tomorrow.'

'Bye then.'

'Bye.'

Andre turned and started heading back to the dorm block, unable to shake the feeling that he'd just accepted an invite to his worst nightmare.

CHAPTER ELEVEN

'Your dad wears a Stetson?' Tilly stared at Andre, her kohl-lined eyes wide with shock.

'And Wranglers with cowboy boots?' Billie said, looking equally stunned.

Andre nodded gloomily. It was the following day and the girls were in his dorm room helping him get ready for his night out with Joe. 'It's how they dress in Texas.'

'I quite like the cowboy look,' Billie said. 'Does he have a big belt buckle? I read an article once that said the bigger the belt buckle, the more pride they have in the cowboy life.'

'What?' Andre stared at her in disbelief.

'Yeah, cowboys have got real swagger.' Tilly

nodded in agreement. 'Does he ride a horse too?'

'What? No! He's not an actual cowboy. He works in the oil industry.'

'Oh.' Tilly started rooting through Andre's tops. 'Maybe you should wear a denim shirt. Have you got anything with rhinestones?'

'Yes, and how about a red bandana around your neck?' Billie said. 'Cowboys wear bandanas round their necks, right?'

'Hold it right there!' Andre exclaimed. 'I am not going out dressed like some cowboy out of *Oklahoma*.'

'Go on!' Tilly said. 'It'll be fun.'

'Yeah,' Billie said. 'It'll be like a fashion tribute to your dad.'

'You don't understand.' Andre sat down on the bed. 'I don't want to be a fashion tribute to him. I don't want to look like him at all.'

'Why not?' Billie put down the bandana she was holding and sat next to him.

'Because I'm not like him – not at all. If you must

know, I'm actually a huge disappointment to him.'

'What?' Tilly dropped her armful of tops and stared at him. 'How could you be a disappointment to him?'

Andre gave a dry laugh. 'Huh, take your pick. Because I'm a dancer. Because I'm a fashionista. Because I'm vegan. Because I'm gay. Basically I'm everything he never wanted in a son.'

'But that's rubbish!' Tilly's face had flushed now, the way it always did before she was about to get angry. 'He should be proud to be your dad.'

'Yeah.' Billie nodded in agreement. 'You're amazing, Dre. You're so talented and you've achieved so much already. Are you sure he feels that way?'

'Oh yeah. You should see the way he looks at me. You know the way Mrs Jones looks at you in tap if you miss a step?'

'Yeah,' both girls chorused. The Mrs Jones Stare was infamous at WEDA.

'Well it's like that but a thousand times worse. It's one of the reasons I work extra hard at the things I love . . . so I never turn out like him.'

'I'd like to meet this dad of yours.' Tilly glared. 'I'd soon put him straight.'

Andre gave her a feeble smile. He'd never really told any of his friends what his dad was like before. He'd been too embarrassed. But seeing Tilly and Billie's outraged reactions was some consolation at least.

'OK. Scrap the father tribute idea,' Tilly said, marching back over to the wardrobe. 'Today's look is going to be all about you.'

'Yes!' Billie leaped up and went over to join her. 'It's gonna be Dre-tastic.'

'I'm thinking teal harem pants,' Tilly said.

'Yes.' Billie nodded. 'And how about one of your signature baseball caps?' She started looking through Andre's collection of headwear and pulled out a cap with BORN BEAUTIFUL written in diamante around the rim. 'This one is Andre through and through.'

'And black patent Docs,' Tilly said, pulling out a

pair of DMs. 'You can show that loser dad of yours that cowboy boots are so last century.'

Andre laughed. Usually he hated the thought of anyone else styling him – unless it was Vivienne Westwood, of course – but this felt great. It was as if Tilly and Billie were putting his confidence back together along with his outfit.

By the time he arrived in London Andre was back to his fabulous defiant self. He was going to show his dad what he was all about if it killed him. And maybe if he did it with enough swag he'd be able to pull it off. After all, his dad had said that today was all about Andre and getting to know him better.

Earlier in the day, Andre had got his mum to tell Joe that he'd really like to see the musical *Matilda*. Joe had managed to get a couple of last-minute tickets for the matinee and they'd arranged to meet outside the theatre. As Andre crossed the street he saw Joe's hulking figure leaning against the theatre wall. He was wearing a denim jacket over a denim shirt . . . with jeans and a big belt buckle in the shape of a steer head. Andre had never seen so much denim on one person. This wasn't just a fashion faux pas, it was a fashion fatality. He adjusted his baseball cap and walked over.

'Hey, Dad.'

'Hey, son.' Joe looked him up and down.

Don't you dare say anything rude about my clothes, Andre thought to himself. *Not when you're wearing triple denim.*

'So, shall we go in?' Joe nodded to the theatre doors.

'Sure.' Andre breathed a sigh of relief and followed him inside.

After a few minutes of awkward small talk about the weather in the UK and the joys of travelling on the Underground, the theatre lights dimmed. Andre always got goose-bumps at the beginning of a show. He thought of the performers waiting nervously in the wings. He imagined he was one of them. He couldn't wait until this was his life – performing in front of crowds on a regular basis. It was what he was born to do.

As soon as the show began Andre forgot all about his dad and any awkwardness and lost himself in the performance. He wished that real life could be like a musical; that it could be perfectly acceptable to break into a song and dance whenever you felt like it. It would be so much more fun. Andre pictured himself up on the stage, dancing his heart out just like the cast of young dancers in *Matilda*, wowing a West-End audience. His dad shifted in the seat next to him. Then he coughed. Then he yawned. Andre's skin began to prickle. What was his problem? Why was he acting bored? How could he not enjoy the talent on display? Was he made of stone? Andre took a deep breath and tried to focus on the show. But he couldn't concentrate. Now all he could think about was his dumb-ass dad.

For the rest of the performance Joe kept fidgeting and coughing and yawning. At one point – the most dramatic point – he even gave a loud sigh. When it was time for the cast to take their bows he only clapped his hands together twice – Andre was counting. As they made their way out of the theatre and on to the street Andre looked longingly in the direction of the station. He just wanted to get on the first train out of there – he didn't care where it was going.

'So,' Joe said. 'Shall we go get something to eat? I'm starving.'

Andre sighed. He supposed he ought to. It would look a bit rude if he just bailed at this point but Joe had better not say anything mean about the show. 'OK.'

'Let's look down here.' Joe started heading off along the street. Andre had to run to keep up with his stride.

'How 'bout this place?' Joe said, pointing to a steak house. But it clearly wasn't really a question because before Andre could answer he'd opened the door and gone inside.

So much for this being all about Andre and what

he liked. He trudged after Joe into the darkened restaurant. It was chain-style Americana, with a juke box and booths and framed baseball shirts on the wall. It was the kind of restaurant that made Andre cringe.

A waitress showed them to a table by the window and gave them both menus. Andre scanned through the sea of meat options. The only thing he could eat here was a tomato salad. Great. To make matters worse, the smell of steak was making his stomach growl. But there was no way he was going to cave now, especially not in front of his dad.

'What would you like?' Joe asked, placing his menu down.

'I'll have the tomato salad.'

Joe sighed. 'Come on, son. We're in a steak house.'

'Yes. And I'm vegan.'

Joe gave an even heavier sigh.

Andre felt in his pocket for the piece of rose quartz Raf had given him and held it tightly. He hoped Raf had been right about the properties of the stone. He needed all the extra strength he could get right now.

After a few minutes of yet more awkward silence the waitress returned to their table.

'Are you guys ready to order?' she asked in a sing-song voice.

'Yes, I'll have a T-bone steak – extra rare,' Joe said, looking straight at Andre.

'And I'll have the tomato salad, with no dressing,' Andre said, equally defiantly, still clutching the rose quartz. It was a battle of wills, menu style – a battle he was not going to lose.

'So, what did you think of the show?' Andre asked, as soon as the waitress had left.

'It was all right.' Joe took off his jacket and leaned back in his chair. 'Not my kind of music, though. I'm more of a country and western fan myself.'

No kidding, Andre thought drily, trying not to shudder.

'I mean, musicals are a bit lame, aren't they?' Joe took a sip of his beer.

'Why?' Andre stared across the table at him. How the hell did he and this man share the same gene pool?

'Well, it's not as if we all start singing and dancing every couple of minutes in real life, is it? It's kinda unrealistic.'

'It's not supposed to be realistic,' Andre replied. 'It's entertainment. It's artistic expression. It's –'

'It's baloney is what it is,' Joe interrupted with a grin.

Andre felt time slowing down to a snail-like crawl. He wondered if he could fake an excuse to leave. Maybe he could pretend to have food poisoning – but they hadn't eaten yet. He looked around the restaurant for inspiration. Maybe he could pretend he was having an allergic reaction to the lame-o stars and stripes wallpaper.

'So, son, I've been thinking.'

Uh-oh, this sounded ominous. 'Yes?'

'Maybe the reason we don't always see eye to eye is because we've never had the chance to 'properly get to know one another.'

'Maybe,' Andre replied. But he had a horrible feeling that if they got to know one another better they'd only get along even worse.

'So, I was wonderin' if maybe you'd like to come to Texas for the summer. Hang out at the ranch.' Joe took a swig from his bottle of beer. 'Do an internship at Hackett Oil.'

'Do a what at what?' Andre stared at him, horrified.

'An internship. Get to see the family business from the inside. See if ya might one day want to work with your old man.'

'What old man?' Andre was so shocked he could barely think straight.

'Your dad. *Me!*' Joe grinned at him. 'Your granddaddy did the same for me when I was your age. And now look at me – I'm running the whole company.'

Andre took a deep breath. 'You want me to come and work at Hackett Oil?'

'Of course. It's a family business. Been passed down for generations now.'

'But – but I'm a dancer.'

Joe laughed. 'But dance isn't a proper career, is it? I know your mom got lucky and made a success of it, but most dancers don't ever hit the big time.'

Andre's face flushed. 'My mum didn't get lucky. She worked her butt off to get where she did. And that's what I'm going to do too.'

Joe sighed. 'There's more to life than being famous, you know. A lot more.'

'I know.'

'Really?' Joe cleared his throat. 'Look, son, I'm not trying to be a party-pooper but someone needs to talk some sense into you. You need a career with prospects, something solid to build a life on.'

'That's what I've got.' Andre's body tensed. He couldn't believe what he was hearing.

'Life isn't one big musical. It's a dog eat dog world out there.'

Andre frowned at him. 'I thought this evening was supposed to be about me.'

'It is. That's why I'm saying all of this. I'm trying to talk some sense into you.'

'No – you're trying to control me.' Andre's voice rose. The diners at the tables next to them turned to stare but he didn't care.

'I'm not trying to control you.' Joe leaned forwards, his voice lowered. 'I'm trying to help you.'

Anger began bubbling in the pit of Andre's stomach. 'You said you wanted to get to know me better.'

'I do.'

'No, you want to try to change me into a . . . a cow-eating, triple-denim-wearing oil man. You want me to give up on my dreams and sell my soul to the devil.'

Joe gave another of his sighs. 'No, I want you to wake up from your dreams and smell the coffee, son.'

'Oh, please.'

The waitress arrived back at their table and placed their meals in front of them. Joe's steak was so rare Andre could see the blood oozing from it. He felt sick to his stomach.

'Enjoy your meal,' the waitress trilled, blissfully unaware of the cloud of anger hanging over the table.

'I'm a dancer, Dad,' Andre said as soon as the waitress left. 'It's in my blood. It's not a fad, it's not about getting famous, it's about doing what I love and if you can't accept that there's no point to this.' Andre's anger faded, replaced by crushing disappointment. He couldn't believe he'd been stupid enough to think that Joe might actually have wanted to get to know the real him; that this night could have actually been a success. He shoved the rose quartz back in his pocket, stood up and grabbed his jacket from the back of his chair.

Joe frowned at him. 'Where are you going?'

'I'm going home. Because WEDA is my home,

Dad. It's where I belong. Enjoy your cow carcass.'

He looked pointedly at Joe's plate.

'Andre, please.'

'Just leave me alone.' And with that, Andre raced to the door.

CHAPTER
TWELVE

Andre stumbled from the restaurant and started running along the crowded street. He didn't know where he was going and he didn't care, he just had to get away from his dad. Finally, he stopped in a shop doorway to catch his breath. He felt as if he'd been ambushed, lured to London by the promise of a musical and some father-son bonding time, only to be beaten over the head by his dad's refusal to accept him for who he was. How could Joe think that Andre would ever want to work in the oil industry? Didn't he know him at all? And then the horrible truth hit home – he didn't. His own father didn't know him at all. And even worse, he didn't *want* to know him. He just wanted to turn him into a denim-clad clone of himself.

Andre looked along the road. The pavement was crowded with weary-looking commuters on their way home from work. Andre shuddered. The thought of having to go to the same job at the same time, day in and day out, filled him with dread. He wanted to be free to live life on his terms. Then he Spotted an old man walking towards him through the crowd. He had long white hair and a wispy white beard and was wearing a floor-length, red velvet cloak. He looked awesome – like a wizard. As the man got closer Andre saw that he had ornate silver rings on his fingers and he was holding an elaborately carved cane. Andre's skin began to tingle. This was what he loved most about London – people could dress however they wanted. They could *be* whoever they wanted. Now Andre's whole body was tingling. *He* could be whoever he wanted. Joe couldn't control him. His life was his own to create. As long as he was following his heart and doing what made it sing, he'd be happy. Andre grinned and set off down the road in the same direction as the wizard.

The next day was the first day of rehearsals for the Cool Earth show. Andre had called a meeting of all the cast members in the Murphy Studio. Still feeling pumped from his realization the night before, he decided to give them all a pep talk based on the ethos behind the charity. He'd once read an article about Ted Talks which said that the first ten seconds of a speech were vital. If you didn't win the audience's attention then you'd probably lost them for good.

'The world is going to end,' Andre declared, as soon as all the students were assembled and sitting on the studio floor. He counted to five in his head to allow for a dramatic enough pause. 'The world is going to end . . . unless we all pull together to save it.' Satisfied that he had their attention he went on to talk about the work Cool Earth was doing to save the rainforests and therefore the planet. 'This is our chance to show how dancing can unite the world,'

Andre finished. 'It's our chance to save the world from extinction.'

To his delight, the dancers all burst into applause – led by Tilly whooping and yelling. Andre handed out rehearsal schedules for each of the different dances. Rehearsals would be taking place every evening after school and all over the weekends until the show. Andre would be choreographing all of them. It meant that Andre had no spare time until the show but he wasn't complaining. He was doing what he loved and, after his nightmare dinner with his dad and nearly being abducted into the oil industry, he couldn't have felt any luckier.

'Before you guys go, I'd like you to freestyle to one of the songs I've picked for the show,' Andre said, flicking through the playlist on Tilly's phone. 'Just do whatever comes naturally, really let yourself go.' He pressed play and 'Right Here, Right Now' by Fatboy Slim started booming around the studio.

Andre watched as the students began to dance. 'Dance as if the world depends upon it!' he yelled in encouragement. 'Because it does!'

He started weaving his way between the dancers looking for ideas. Raf and MJ were involved in some kind of capoeira duo. Tilly's room-mate Naomi was pulling some really impressive acrobatic moves. Other dancers, led by Cassandra, were spinning in pirouettes. Andre pictured them in leotards accessorized with strips of fabric that would fly out as they spun. His head filled with a palette of blue and silver and gold. He saw the stage filling with dancers – the word UNITE being projected above them. As the song built the dancers became more animated and Andre's mind filled with more images and ideas. Endangered species, indigenous people, clouds, a butterfly. Then he saw himself, emerging in the middle of them, dressed as Apollo, in a tribute to King Louis XIV, wearing a huge, sun-style headdress. Andre grinned. Spotted wasn't the only way he could channel his inner fashionista – he could do it through performance too. And the best thing about styling a dance show was that he didn't have to worry about haters or numbers of likes. The song came to an end and one by one the dancers fell still.

'Guys, that was awesome! Thank you so much,' Andre exclaimed. 'See you all in rehearsals soon.' He hurried over to his bag and took out a notebook and pen. He had a head full of inspiration and he didn't want to lose any of it.

At lunch Andre met with Il Bello in the Stable Studio to brainstorm ideas for the show.

'How did it go with your dad?' Tilly asked as soon as he walked in. They hadn't had a chance to catch up before the rehearsal.

'Not so good,' Andre replied. 'He tried to get me to go and work with him in Texas.'

'What?' Billie stared at him.

'I know, right? He wants me to work in the oil industry. Me!' Andre exclaimed.

Raf started to laugh. 'What the hell? Why would he want you to do that?'

'Because he wants me to be exactly like him

and he can't handle it that I'm not.' Andre sighed. 'Thanks for that rose quartz, by the way. It came in very handy last night. It definitely made me feel stronger.' He reached into his pocket for the crystal and offered it to Raf. 'Here, do you want it back?'

Raf shook his head. 'No, bro, it was a gift. Keep it till someone else needs it more, then pass it on.' He sighed. 'Dads, eh? Well, if it's any consolation, my dad always wanted me to be a boxer. He still buys me boxing gear for my birthday each year.'

'Are you OK?' Tilly said, coming over and giving Andre's hand a squeeze.

'Yeah. I just need to forget it ever happened. From now on, I'm an orphan.' Andre gave another dramatic sigh.

'You still have a mum!' Tilly said.

'Yeah, a really cool mum,' Billie added.

'OK, I'm half an orphan,' Andre replied.

'Well, you know what they say,' Tilly said with a grin.

'What?' Andre looked at her.

'If you have a broken heart you've got to fix it with art.'

'Love it!' Andre grinned back. 'So let's fix my heart – let's get this show nailed.'

For the rest of lunchbreak Andre bounced his ideas off Il Bello, with Tilly drawing sketches and Billie making notes and Raf and MJ chiming in with ideas for music and lighting and background projections. Like a series of polaroid pictures, each of the dances was becoming more and more defined in his head.

'This is going to be epic!' Tilly exclaimed as she made the finishing touches to her sketch of the final scene.

Andre felt a stab of pride. It *was* going to be epic. He'd show his dad he wasn't a waste of space; that his dreams actually meant something.

That evening, Andre went to his mum's apartment for dinner.

'I hear things with your dad didn't go so well,' she said as soon as he came in.

'Yeah, you could say that.' Andre followed her into the kitchen and helped himself to a banana from the fruit bowl. 'It was an ambush, Mum.'

Miss Murphy frowned. 'What do you mean?'

'He asked me if I'd like to work in the oil industry with him!'

'He did what?' Miss Murphy's eyes glinted with indignation.

'He said I needed to get a proper job – that dancing wasn't secure, it wouldn't pay the bills.'

Miss Murphy laughed. 'Well, I seemed to do all right.'

'Apparently you just got lucky.'

'*What?*' Miss Murphy looked really mad now.

'Don't worry, I set him straight. Mum, can I ask you something?'

'Of course, my love.'

'Please, can you promise me there'll be no more surprise father-son bonding visits? I can only take so much awkwardness – not to mention all the denim – in one lifetime.'

'Sure.' Miss Murphy laughed again but she looked sad. She switched on the kettle and popped two ginger teabags into mugs. 'I'm so sorry it didn't work out, Andre. I never would have suggested it if I thought he was going to do that. I just wanted to do something that would make you feel better.'

'It's OK. To be honest, I'm feeling great.'

'You are?' She studied his face with her mum x-ray vision.

'Yeah. I'm so enjoying choreographing for the Cool Earth show. It's therapeutic putting my feelings into my art.'

'And I'm so proud of how you're getting on. Seriously. In fact . . .' Miss Murphy opened the cupboard by the sink and took out Andre's laptop and phone. 'I think it's time you had these back. As long as you promise me you won't let it get out of control again.'

'Oh. Right. OK.' As Andre took the devices from her the weirdest thing happened. Instead of feeling excited or relieved he felt uneasy. Life had ended up being so much simpler without online access . . . and so much happier. He shoved them in his backpack and decided not to think about them until after dinner. Maybe he'd feel differently later.

But when Andre got back to his room that evening his uneasiness about going back online had grown. He placed his laptop and phone on his bed and stared at them nervously as if they were ticking time-bombs. As soon as he turned them on he'd get notifications coming through. What if there'd been more negative comments on Spotted? What if @snarkerella had been trolling his social media accounts? He could feel himself start to slide back down the internet rabbit hole again. He picked up his devices, went down the corridor to Tilly's room and knocked on the door.

Tilly opened the door wearing a plastic bag on

her head, which could only mean one thing – she was dying her hair again.

'Dre! Oh my God, you got your phone back! That's amazing.'

'Is it, though?' Andre came in and sat down on her bed. The room reeked of hair dye. 'Tillz, can I ask you a favour?'

'Of course.'

'Could you take care of these for me tonight?' He placed his laptop and phone on the bed.

Tilly looked at him like he was insane. 'But why?'

'I'm not sure I'm ready to go back online yet. I really want to get a good night's sleep before all the rehearsals begin. I don't want to have to worry about haters and stuff.'

'Oh, Dre, of course.' Tilly took his laptop and phone and put them in her cupboard. 'I'll tell you what. How about the crew are all with you when you do decide to go back online? To give you moral support.'

Andre nodded and his feeling of uneasiness

started to fade. 'That would be awesome. Thank you.'

'No problem. Now go and get some sleep. I need to wash my hair.' Tilly bundled him over to the door. 'I'm dying it scarlet and black for the show,' she explained.

'That sounds great.' Andre hugged her good night. 'Thanks so much for reconfiscating my phone, Tillz.'

Tilly laughed. 'That's what friends are for.'

CHAPTER THIRTEEN

The next morning, Andre woke up early, refreshed and raring to go. He glanced across the room. MJ's bed was empty; he must have gone for a run. Andre quickly got ready – which for him meant only taking half an hour on his hair – and went to the canteen. He got a breakfast smoothie from the juice bar and a plate of scrambled tofu. As he glanced around for somewhere to sit he saw the rest of Il Bello all hunched over a table in the far corner, deep in conversation. Even Billie was there and she never normally made it to breakfast as she was a non-boarder and had so far to come. Andre frowned. Why hadn't MJ woken him? Had they called a crew meeting without him? He made his way over to the table.

'Dre!' Billie cried as soon as she saw him. 'Look, guys, he's here.'

'What's going on?' Andre asked.

'Emergency meeting,' Tilly explained. Her hair looked amazing – jet black with bright red tips.

'Without me?' Andre began to pout.

'No, *about* you,' Tilly said. 'What do you think of my hair? Do you think it'll look good for the show?'

'Yeah, it looks fetch,' Andre muttered, sitting down. 'But why are you meeting about me?'

'We've made you something.' Billie's eyes gleamed with excitement.

'To help make your transition back to the online world a happy and successful one,' MJ said, before taking a bite of toast.

Raf nodded and smiled.

'What do you mean?'

Tilly placed Andre's laptop and phone on the table.

'Before you go back online we want you to

read this.' Billie handed Andre a sheet of paper. Tilly had drawn a cartoon of Andre in his BORN BEAUTIFUL baseball cap on one side of the page, next to a list written in Billie's curly handwriting.

HANDLING THE HATERS

1. Haters gonna hate . . . but creators gonna create. Be proud that you've a creator.

2. Haters are jealous. Be proud that you've achieved something to make them jealous.

3. Haters are slayed by the three Bs: Be fearless. Be authentic. Be you!

4. Haters are energy vampires. Don't let them drain you.

5. Haters are unhappy at heart. Pity them, don't let them hurt you.

6. Haters can be beaten by two simple words: BLOCK and DELETE.

7. Haters feed off fear and recognition. Don't feed the trolls!

8. Haters can fuel your passions. Turn your fear into fire.

9. Haters are stuck in negativity. You are free to dream.

10. Haters can't compete with confidence. As your hero Vivienne Westwood says: 'Confidence is the best fashion accessory.'

'Oh my God, guys, this is amazing!' Andre exclaimed.

'Do you like it?' Billie looked at him anxiously. 'We don't want you to go back to how you were before the detox. We want you to stay happy.'

'Yeah, bro,' Raf said, putting his hand on Andre's shoulder. 'You can't let the haters win.'

'I won't.' Andre re-read the list, then he looked over at his phone.

'Are you ready?' Tilly asked.

Andre nodded. Tilly pushed the phone across the table to him and he turned it on. His notifications started pinging. Andre looked back at the list Il Bello had made for him. He had this. He wasn't scared of some stupid online troll any more. He wasn't going to let them get to him. He was a creator and proud. He scanned his inbox.

'Oh shoot.'

'What is it? Has that idiot trolled you again?' Tilly said with a frown. 'If they have I swear I'm gonna hunt them down and –'

'No. It's my dad. He sent me an email the other night – after our London nightmare.' Andre read the title of the email. It simply said, HOWDY. He quickly scanned the rest of his emails and checked his social media accounts. There was nothing from @snarkerella. There were no more horrible posts on Spotted either. In fact, since he'd been on digital detox the blog had gained five more followers.

'So, what did your dad say?' Billie asked.

'He better not be chatting rubbish about your dancing again,' Tilly practically snarled.

Andre laughed. 'Don't even joke about it. OK, here goes . . .' He clicked the email open.

Howdy son,

I just wanted to say I'm really sorry for the way things went the other evening. I'm not the greatest when it comes to expressing how I feel but I'm your dad and I want you to know that I love you. And I always will. I guess I was hoping for the chance to get to hang out some more. But I wasn't trying to control you. And if you want to be a dancer I respect your wishes. I seem to be stuck in my ways sometimes and for that I am truly sorry. So I'll see you next time you're in the States. I promise I won't make you come to work with me – or sell your soul to the devil.

Dad

'What did he say?' Billie asked.

Andre read them the email. 'Now I feel kind of bad,' he said. 'He doesn't know about the digital detox. He must think I'm ignoring him.'

'Reply to him now,' Billie said. Then her eyes lit

up. 'I know – why don't you invite him to the show?'

'What?' Andre stared at her.

'It sounds as if he might finally be ready to accept you for who you are. I bet if he saw what you're capable of he'd be so proud.'

'Oh, I don't know. I don't think it's his kind of thing. You should have seen what he was like watching *Matilda*. It was as though he was having his teeth pulled and leg hair waxed – at the same time.'

'But the Cool Earth show isn't going to be anything like *Matilda*,' Tilly said. 'It's going to be way edgier.'

Andre looked to MJ and Raf.

'I say go for it,' Raf said.

'Yeah.' MJ agreed. 'Ask him to come.'

'OK then . . .' Andre hit reply and began to type.

Hey Dad,

Thanks for your email and sorry it's taken me a while to respond. I've been on a digital detox. Long story. Anyway, there's this show I'm choreographing and dancing in.

It's happening in London in about a month.

I know you've only just been to the UK and

you'll probably be busy with work and all

but, you know, if you wanted to come back

for the show I'd be glad to see you. Just let

Mum know and she can sort you out a ticket.

OK. See you.

Andre

Andre took a swig of his smoothie and smiled. Even though he knew it was highly unlikely his dad would come back to see the show it felt good to clear the air. And at least now he had it in writing that his dad wouldn't abduct him and force him into a life of denim, cowboy boots and oil. He looked down at his phone. It was so great to be free from the curse of wanting to check it all the time. He was back in control again and it was the best feeling in the world.

CHAPTER
FOURTEEN

The next few weeks raced by in a blur of rehearsals, costume design and choreography. Andre had never been so busy. But instead of feeling drained he was energised – fuelled by the excitement of seeing his visions slowly become a reality. Working with the students and teachers of WEDA to create and choreograph the show was helping him feel fulfilled. He felt like he was discovering his true calling as an artist, like he had real purpose in life outside of the online world. When the day of the Cool Earth show arrived Andre lay there, waiting until his alarm clock oh-so-slowly ticked round to five, then he leaped out of bed. He'd barely slept a wink all night – he was way too nervous and excited, or nerve-cited as Billie called it. A coach would be arriving to take the WEDA students to Sadler's Wells straight after breakfast to do one final tech rehearsal before the show. Andre got out of bed and stared at MJ, who was still fast asleep. How could he sleep at a time like this?

Andre marched over and shook his shoulder. 'How can you sleep at a time like this?' he hissed.

MJ blinked at his alarm clock. 'It's five o'clock,' he mumbled. 'I'm supposed to sleep at a time like this.'

'It's the day of the show,' Andre said. 'I need you to get up. We need to be prepared.'

MJ groaned. 'But it isn't time to get up.'

'Do you think that's what Nureyev said, when he was principal dancer in *Swan Lake*? Do you think Gene Kelly had lie-ins while he was filming *Singing in the Rain*? Seriously, MJ, you need to sort out your attitude.' Andre pulled on his tracksuit. He was so hyped it was like he'd downed five espressos. 'I'm going to wake the others. I expect you to be up and dressed by the time I get back.'

Two hours later, Andre and a bleary-eyed Tilly started loading the costumes on to the coach. They'd been up late into the night making final adjustments but Andre still wasn't sure if they were totally on point.

'Do you think we added enough fabric to the leotards?' he asked. 'Should we have added glitter to the masks? And what about Cassandra's tutu? Is it too gold? Or maybe it isn't enough gold. Is it enough gold?'

Tilly sighed. 'OK, Dre, you're gonna need to take a chill pill.' She placed her hands on his shoulders and stared him in the eyes. 'Seriously. It's going to be great.'

A sudden wave of self-doubt rushed through Andre. 'But . . . but what if it isn't?' he whispered.

Tilly took hold of his arm and gave it a squeeze. 'You were born to do this, Dre. It's going to be awesome.

*

The technical rehearsal did nothing to calm Andre's nerves. The projections kept jumping and they couldn't seem to get the brightness right for the lights during the final dance. By the time it was over Andre was so tense he could barely speak.

'It's going to be OK,' Billie reassured him, as they gathered in the dressing room to get ready. 'That's what rehearsals are for – to iron out all the glitches.'

Andre nodded, his stomach churning. He really hoped she was right.

The door opened and Miss Murphy poked her head in. 'Break a leg, guys,' she said with a smile.

'Thanks, Mum. Any sign of Dad?'

Miss Murphy shook her head. 'No. I guess his flight must have been delayed.'

Yeah, or he had second thoughts about coming. Andre sighed. He couldn't let Joe get to him now – he had way more important things to worry about.

The bell rang. It was three minutes to curtain call. Andre's throat tightened.

'I'd better get to my seat,' Miss Murphy said. She

kissed Andre on the top of his head. 'Love you,' she whispered – and then she was gone.

Andre quickly gathered all of the dancers together in a large circle backstage. 'Thank you so much, guys, for working so hard and putting your trust in me,' he said. 'Let's go out there and make a real difference. But before we do that we have to stay true to the break-a-leg tradition!'

The dancers all held hands and stood on one leg. Then, led by Andre, they hopped up and down three times.

'One . . . two . . . three,' they called in time. 'Break a leg!' They let go of each other's hands and flung their arms in the air.

'Now we're ready,' Andre said with a grin.

Andre stepped out on to the darkened stage and a hush fell over the auditorium. As 'A Change is Gonna Come' began to play, a single spotlight fell upon Andre, pooling him in a stark white light. He was wearing a simple black and white tracksuit with plain black high-tops. The theme was tribal chic with a modern twist. Billie and Tilly had convinced him to keep his look as stripped back as possible. 'So that you can show how life has scarred you,' Tilly explained, 'and let your true self shine.'

Andre's heart pounded hard as he started to move to the rhythm. He felt weird and exposed without his usual fashion mask to hide behind. But the auditorium was so dark and the spotlight so bright that he couldn't see a single person in the crowd. He took a deep breath. It was time to let his dancing do the talking. He needed to channel all of the pain – both his and the world's – through his body and mind. He and Mr Marlo had worked hard on the choreography for this piece. Now it all came together. Andre crouched and slowly snaked up, keeping his eyes closed and connecting to the music. Then he started contorting his body to the rhythm in fluid, street-inspired contemporary moves – spinning in an attitude, stretching into an arabesque and then breaking into an emotional section of body popping and waving. As the words of the song wove their way into his movements he thought of how badly he'd longed for change in his own life. How he'd longed to be accepted – by his dad and the world. He thought of all the indigenous people and endangered species and poured their suffering into his dance too. Then he danced as if he were the earth itself – longing to be healed and saved from destruction. As the song built in a crescendo he broke into a section of krumping, using his anger and frustration, then skipped across the stage into a back hand spring back tuck, extending and fanning his legs out at the top like an albatross spreading its wings. He was lost in the music and he felt strong like an eco-warrior. He nailed every six step and stall and he finally remembered what it felt like to feel proud to be him. Then the song faded, the spotlight dimmed and Andre ran from the stage into the wings.

'You were amazing!' Billie said, grabbing him in a hug.

'Yeah, bro,' Raf said, with a high five. 'You kept it real and slayed it out there.'

'Now it's your turn,' Andre said, breathlessly, his nerves now transformed into adrenalin. He turned to the crowd of dancers gathered behind Raf and Billie. 'You've got this, guys.'

'Million Reasons' by Lady Gaga started playing and the dancers made their way on to the stage. Andre watched from the wings as they began their routine. The pieces of silver, gold and bronze cloth attached to their leotards sparkled and shone in the light. It was incredible to see something that had begun as the seed of an idea in his mind brought to life like this. It made him realize that anything was possible if you just dared to dream.

'Hey, Dre,' Tilly whispered as she came and stood next to him. She was wearing a green unitard with pink leopard spots and pictures of toucans. The reflective material shone like a beacon every time the light hit it. She handed him his BORN BEAUTIFUL baseball cap and some gold chains.

Il Bello were dancing next and he needed to accessorize.

'Wow, look at Billie and Raf,' Tilly whispered.

Andre watched as Raf lifted Billie in a perfect split above his head. The strips of fabric attached to Billie's leotard flickered in the air like ticker-tape as Raf spun her round. There was a ripple of applause from the crowd as Raf and Billie dropped into a swan dive and shared a powerful embrace. Then the music ended and the lights faded. Billie and Raf came racing off the stage and a couple of wardrobe assistants set to work, helping them quickly change into their street gear. The other dancers all filed past them back to the dressing rooms. Andre gathered Il Bello in a group hug.

'Be fearless. Be authentic. Be you,' they quietly chanted, before walking on to the stage.

'Human' by Rag'n'Bone Man began to play and golden spotlights circled. As Andre danced he thought of how hard he'd fought to get WEDA and his mum to accept street dance. Now, not only was street dance on the curriculum at WEDA, but his crew were representing WEDA at Sadler's Wells. Elation erupted from his body in every pop and spin. Then, annoyingly, an image of his dad appeared in his head. If only Joe would accept him for who he truly was. If only he'd bothered to come to the show. Andre channelled his disappointment into his dance. Faster and faster he bent back, stretching his arm back again and again in his African dance moves until his joy and disappointment blended together in a perfect storm. And then there was a moment of stillness. Andre's heart thumped in his rib cage, his chest rising and falling violently as he tried to catch his breath. Just as the song said, he was only human. He could only do his best and if that wasn't good enough for his dad well then too bad.

The lights cut to black and Il Bello rushed from the stage to deafening applause. Cassandra was waiting in the wings, her face perfectly composed beneath her mask, her gaze focused. She and the other ballet dancers were dressed in unitards with a geometric print and blue tutus woven with gold, all topped off with black masks and black pointe shoes. A wardrobe assistant pulled Andre off to the back of the wing as the dancers filed on to the stage. It was time for his big costume change.

'Don't Let the Sun Go Down on Me' began to play and Andre shivered as he thought of King Louis XIV hundreds of years ago, preparing to dance for the French court as a teenage boy. He thought of the courage it must have taken for King Louis to be true to himself and his passion for dance. And now here Andre was all these centuries later, about to dance his own tribute to the king. He couldn't believe he'd ever dissed history. Now he felt history coursing through his veins. As a wardrobe assistant attached a huge, sun-shaped crown to Andre's head he grinned. *This one's for you, King Louis*, he thought, before making his way to the side of the stage. As soon as he heard his cue Andre erupted on to the stage in the middle of a group of bhangra dancers.

Gasps echoed up from the audience, filling Andre with fearlessness. He was like the sun god Apollo.

Projected images of clouds began drifting over the stage. The image of a butterfly landed on Cassandra's hand as she held a perfect lunge, then it fluttered off up into the clouds, led from her port de bras. Pictures of different endangered animals were projected on to the backdrop of the stage. The dancers moved faster and faster. A riotous mix of capoeira, bhangra and ballet, led by a masked Cassandra, her emotive performance pulling out the best in everyone. Then the beats slowed and everyone lunged into a humble warrior pose with their heads bowed to the ground.

As 'Change' by Christina Aguilera began playing the dancers backed off to the sides of the stage, making way for Naomi, dressed in a unitard decorated in a bright scarlet and orange flame print. Naomi's body contorted this way and that, as she fused traditional Chinese fan dance with contemporary acrobatics, symbolizing the destruction of the world. The flame-red fabric of her fan was like fire burning across the stage, flowing over the other dancers and engulfing Naomi. Even though he'd seen it many times in rehearsal this moment always took Andre's breath away. The combination of the beautiful melody of the song with the destructive, end of the world images choked him up every time. It seemed that the audience felt the same way too, because when the song faded there wasn't a sound.

As soon as the lights blacked out everyone left the stage apart from Raf and MJ. 'Right Here Right Now' by Fatboy Slim began booming out and Raf and MJ started their capoeira duo. Then Andre, still dressed as Apollo, led the other dancers back on. They were now all dressed in different costumes representing the different corners of the globe.

Strobe lights started flashing and for the first time, Andre was able to see the silhouettes of the audience. They were all on their feet, clapping and cheering and dancing along! Andre fed off their energy, using it to fuel his movements. He felt connected to everyone and everything – not just in Sadler's Wells but the whole world. This was what unity looked like – and he never wanted it to end.

As the song died the other dancers crept from the stage and MJ moonwalked into the spotlight. As he did a tribute to his hero Michael Jackson the other dancers frantically got changed in the wings, pulling T-shirts on over their costumes. The lights cut to total darkness and once again, a rapt silence fell upon the auditorium. Andre made his way back on to the darkened stage holding a flashlight. He turned it on and shone a thin beam of red light around the stage. The other dancers filed back on to the stage as Tilly's mural was projected on to the back wall. One by one they walked up and touched the image of the hand. The words WE ARE ONE came up on the wall. And, as the spotlights brightened, the same words were illuminated on the T-shirts of the dancers. Once again Andre felt a shiver of excitement as he saw his vision brought to life. The dancers all stood in a huge semi-circle, facing the audience.

There were a few moments of silence and for an awful moment Andre thought the audience had suddenly fallen asleep. Or maybe . . . But then the room erupted on to their feet into a cacophony of sound. They had been so stunned and touched by the message of the show it had taken a moment for it to sink in! Andre stared in shock. People were yelling and whooping and whistling and cheering. As the house lights came up Andre blinked and stared into the crowd, looking for his mum. He Spotted her in the middle of the front row leaping up and down, clapping her hands. Then Andre saw something that made his heart practically stop beating. It was a man standing next to his mum – a man clad in triple denim, clapping wildly.

'Dad!' Andre mouthed.

Joe mouthed something back but Andre couldn't understand what it was. But the main thing was that he looked happy. He looked more than happy. He looked proud.

Andre nodded to the other dancers, then they all walked to the front of the stage to take their bows. This time when the crowd erupted into applause they almost blew the roof off.

Once they'd taken their bows Andre was about to lead the dancers off when someone came up on to the stage holding a microphone. A pale, petite woman with bright orange hair.

'Oh my God, it's Vivienne Westwood,' Billie said with a gasp in Andre's ear.

'That was wonderful! You were wonderful!' she said into the mic. 'The imagination and passion you just showed was breathtaking.' As she smiled at the row of dancers her gaze met Andre's for a second. 'And I love the King-Louis look,' she added, with a grin. As she turned back to the audience and thanked them for coming Andre stared at Tilly, shell-shocked.

'Vivienne Westwood loves my look!' he said, gaping, unsure if he was dreaming. If he was he didn't ever want to wake up.

CHAPTER FIFTEEN

Backstage was buzzing, all of the pent-up nerves and discipline from weeks of rehearsals released in explosions of chatter and laughter. Andre stood in a corner, dazed, as people flocked over to congratulate him. 'Vivienne Westwood loves my look,' was all he could reply, over and over, like a broken record.

'Andre!' Miss Murphy came hurrying up, her face glowing with excitement. 'That was amazing!' She flung her arms around him and hugged him tightly.

'Thanks, Mum. Did you hear what Vivienne Westwood said? She loves my look. Vivienne Westwood – loves – my – look!'

Miss Murphy laughed. 'And so she should! I'm so proud of you.'

'And so am I, son,' came a gruff voice from over her shoulder.

Andre untangled himself from his mum's embrace to see his dad standing behind her.

'That was something else!' Joe exclaimed. And from the way he was grinning he clearly meant it as a good thing. Andre couldn't be certain but he even thought he might spy a suspicious shimmer to his dad's eyes. 'You're an incredible dancer.'

Andre's face flushed. 'Thanks, Dad.'

'And you really choreographed the whole thing too?'

Andre nodded.

Joe whistled, clearly impressed.

'Isn't he talented?' Miss Murphy said.

'He sure is.' Joe cleared his throat and shifted awkwardly on his feet. 'You know I hadn't realized before just how powerful dance can be. That was – that was awesome.'

Andre grinned. This dream he was living just kept on getting better and better. 'Thanks, Dad.'

'How about we go for a meal together – to celebrate?' Joe looked from Andre to Miss Murphy.

'Can my friends come too?'

'Sure.'

'And can we go to a vegan restaurant this time?'

Joe grimaced but then he began to nod. 'All right.'

'Thanks, Dad. Hey, did you hear what Vivienne Westwood said to me?'

'Tonight has been so surreal,' Andre exclaimed as he watched his dad biting into a vegetable pancake roll.

'Tonight has been the best night of my life,' Tilly said.

The other members of Il Bello all murmured their agreement.

They'd come with Joe and Miss Murphy to a vegan restaurant in Soho.

'I did something for you,' Tilly said, taking her

phone from her bag and moving closer to Andre.

'What?' Andre asked, before taking a mouthful of his vegan sweet and sour.

'I posted something on Spotted. I know you wanted to give blogging a break till after the show so this is a kind of welcome back present.'

'It's really cool,' Billie said, with a grin.

Tilly passed her phone to Andre. She'd written a new blog post on Spotted called 'Your Vibe Attracts Your Tribe'.

Andre's heart filled with happiness as he began to read. There was a series of photos of Il Bello taken in the Stable Studio and then each of them had spoken movingly about how much the crew meant to them and the importance of finding your tribe.

'Guys, this is great!' he said.

He scrolled down to the comments. They were all positive – apart from one.

Ha! Wouldn't want to attract this tribe
of freaks!

As Andre read the words he waited for the usual feelings of anger and dread to creep into him, but there was nothing. Instead, he started to laugh.

'Hmmm, a tribe of freaks . . . sounds like a great name for a new show!' Andre said.

Tonight, he had danced at Sadler's Wells. Tonight, twenty people had performed in a show he had choreographed at Sadler's Wells. Tonight, he'd lived his dream – surrounded by people who loved and accepted him for who he truly was. Even his dad had come through. He glanced down the table to Joe, who was grinning as he picked up chopsticks full of beansprouts. Instead of feeling threatened by the troll Andre felt sad for them. He'd rather be a so-called freak any day of the week than be someone who saw the worst in everything.

'What's up?' Tilly asked. She leaned over to look at the phone. 'Oh no.'

'What is it?' Billie said, instantly looking concerned.

'We got a snarky comment on the blog. I

197

shouldn't have changed the security settings. I just didn't want you to get any extra notifications – I wanted the post to be a surprise.' Tilly put her hand on Andre's arm. 'Don't let them get to you, Dre, they're not worth it.'

'I know.' Andre looked at her and smiled. 'Don't worry. I'm not going to waste another second worrying about the Hoovers.'

Tilly frowned. 'The Hoovers?'

'The people who suck all the joy out of life.'

As Billie and Tilly started laughing Andre looked up the table to Joe. 'Yo, Dad, how are the veggies?'

Joe looked back at him and grinned. 'Ya know what, son? I'm actually enjoyin' them.'

Andre picked up some fried pepper with his chopsticks. That was the thing about life – it was sweet and sour, just like his meal. Bad stuff would always happen and haters would hate, but if enough people focused on creating positive things, then miracles could happen too – miracles like Cool Earth raising enough money to help heal the planet.

Miracles like his steak-loving, macho-man dad eating beansprouts. And miracles like fashion icon Vivienne Westwood saying she loved Andre's look. Yes, as long as Andre focused on the positive and continued to create he would stay immune to any hate. He looked at the table full of the people he loved most in the world and every cell in his body began dancing with joy.

Your Vibe Attracts Your Tribe

Everyone's born beautiful.

But beauty fades in the harsh glare of your

need to be liked.

Don't drown in judgement.

Swim fiercely towards true you choices.

Style is true you armour.

Believe in better, believe in happy.

Open your mind to differences.

Stand strong because you're not the only one.

Someone's out there waiting to be Spotted

just like you.

Be bold and brave enough to be you.

Celebrate life with friends.

Be the first to spread love in life and online,

Because your vibe will attract your tribe,

And your tribe will protect that awesome vibe.

We are One!